Harlequin Romance® brings you
a fresh new story from Australian author

Ally Blake

Curl up and indulge yourself
with this contemporary, vibrant
and heartwarming novel…

Praise for Ally Blake

"Blake's debut book *The Wedding Wish* is an exciting
read. The characters are alive, funny and wonderful."
—*Romantic Times BOOKreviews*

"*The Shock Engagement* by Ally Blake is a read that
will warm the reader's heart and soul…. It's
official! Ally Blake is in my top ten authors list…."
—*www.cataromance.com*

"*A Father in the Making* by Ally Blake has emotional
depth that shows the author's growth and maturity
in her craft. The humor and vitality of this novel is
a joy to behold and I look forward to more. Not a
single thing would I change of this story!"
—*www.cataromance.com*

Dear Reader,

I am as guilty as the next girl of picking up magazines in supermarket queues to find out what the celebrities are up to—which ones are looking glamorous in designer frocks, and which have been caught in compromising photos in which we can see their cellulite.

It got me to thinking—how would it feel if you were a regular gal, a wife and mother, trying to go about the business of raising your kids, but you were married to a famous sportsman? How hard it must be to hold down a normal life with the long lenses of the paparazzi following you and the all-knowing public commenting on your every move.

Out of that thought grew my heroine, Brooke, a woman whose whole adult life has been lived in the public eye. But now that fabulous life has come crashing to a halt; her marriage, her finances, the life she knew are all gone in the blink of an eye. Don't you think it would take some kind of man to stand up for a woman in that position? Especially if he had been her ex-husband's best friend? Ooooh, the plot thickens!!!

I hope you enjoy the twists and turns of *Millionaire to the Rescue* as much as I enjoyed watching them unfold!

Ally
www.allyblake.com

ALLY BLAKE
Millionaire to the Rescue

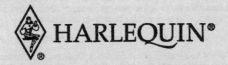

TORONTO • NEW YORK • LONDON
AMSTERDAM • PARIS • SYDNEY • HAMBURG
STOCKHOLM • ATHENS • TOKYO • MILAN • MADRID
PRAGUE • WARSAW • BUDAPEST • AUCKLAND

ISBN-13: 978-0-373-03984-5
ISBN-10:   0-373-03984-0

MILLIONAIRE TO THE RESCUE

First North American Publication 2007.

Having once been a professional cheerleader, **Ally Blake**'s motto is "Smile and the world smiles with you." One way to make Ally smile is sending her on vacations, especially to locations which inspire her writing. New York and Italy are by far her favorite destinations. Other things that make her smile are the gracious city of Melbourne, the gritty Collingwood football team and her gorgeous husband, Mark.

Reading romance novels was a smile-worthy pursuit from long back. So, with such valuable preparation already behind her, Ally wrote and sold her first book. Her career as a writer also gives her a perfectly reasonable excuse to indulge in her stationery addiction. That alone is enough to keep her grinning every day!

Ally would love you to visit her at her Web site, www.allyblake.com.

To a whole team of men
who bring me agony and ecstasy year in
and year out, the Collingwood Football Club.
Go Pies!

CHAPTER ONE

BROOKE'S HEAD hurt. Her heart felt as if it were stampeding through her chest. And all she could see was darkness.

The mix of sounds—a phone ringing a few rooms away, a woman laughing, a muted television—negated the idea that she was dead. Unless, of course, her personal hell meant being forced to listen to the sports channel for the rest of time.

She took stock. She was horizontal with tiny lumps of knotted carpet digging into the skin at the back of her bare arms and calves. Her eyes were closed, hence the general darkness, though it was daytime. She could tell by the blood-red colour filtering through the thin skin of her eyelids.

If she just opened her eyes she would know where she was. But a little voice in the back of her head warned her she wouldn't like it if she did.

Maybe she ought to just lie there for a little while. Blissfully ignorant. Since wherever she was, it was cool. Nobody was hollering at her to take them to soccer practice, or to buy them a new Wiggles toy, or hiding in the bushes to take her photo as she left the gym with no make-up. And, wherever she was, it smelled wonderful. Sharp. Like concentrated citrus. She took a deep breath through her nose. Delicious.

In time the instinct not to slowly expire lying on some random piece of carpet won out, and Brooke opened her eyes.

A face filled her vision completely. A male face with solemn brown eyes, hair the colour of expensive dark chocolate and a sensuously carved mouth she just *knew* looked even more devastating on the rare times it smiled. But it wasn't smiling now. In fact it looked positively uneasy.

'Danny?' she said, her voice hoarse.

'Brooke,' he said, breathing out a wave of relief so strong it tickled her eyelashes. She blinked away the sensation and when she made eye contact again she saw that the unusual abundance of concern in his eyes had faded, leaving her with…nothing. Yep, it was Danny all right.

She cleared her throat. 'Why am I on the floor?'

He pressed his hand to her forehead, first the back and then the palm. So cool. So gentle. So unexpectedly tender. *Do that some more,* she thought, giving in and letting her eyes fall closed once more. *It feels just like heaven.*

'You fainted,' he said softly, as though she might disappear in a puff of smoke if he was his usual intractable self.

Then his words filtered through the haze. She had fainted? She sucked in a deep breath through her nose and was once again caught in a wave of citrus. This time she recognised the sharp, tangy scent as Danny's aftershave. Funny she'd never noticed it before. It was truly drinkable.

'Don't be ridiculous,' she said. 'Fainting's for damsels in distress, Beatles fans and schoolgirls. I'm none of the above and therefore *I* did not faint.'

She sat up to prove her theory and her brain shifted backwards and thumped against a whole world of hurt at the back of her skull. She let out a groan and held her open palm over her eyes to find it was trembling.

Danny shifted to sit on the floor beside her, his sizeable form displacing the air at her left. The carpet fibres would make a mess of his beautiful suit pants. He always wore such nice suits. Stylish, sophisticated and always black. But she couldn't find the words to tell him as much, for when he draped a strong arm across her shoulders, his warm fingers pressing into her bare upper arm, holding her steady, holding her close, it seemed a wise decision to just shut up and lean into his embrace. His unanticipated warmth. His tangible strength. All the better to keep herself from falling.

'Well, either you fainted or you decided to take an ill-advised catnap on the floor of my office,' Danny said, his dry, mocking voice rumbling close to her ear.

His office? Brooke moved her hand away from her eyes. Signed photos of the world's major sportsmen littered the red feature wall behind his huge oak desk. Bookshelves overspilling with priceless memorabilia, hard cover biographies and sports periodicals stood tall and imposing to her right. Three separate televisions embedded into one wall were permanently set to satellite sports channels. So she was in Danny's office at the Good Sports Agency. Odd.

She glanced sideways to find his face mere inches from hers. His eyes boring into hers. Golden-brown they were, the mercurial colour of autumn leaves. Infamously intense and infinitely unsettling. It was a gaze that terrified football club presidents, bamboozled journalists and bewitched women the country over. And as usual she had no idea what was going on behind their depths.

She blinked, looked away and lifted her heavy arm to motion towards the rough coffee-coloured carpet. 'Why did I...you know...lie down?'

'You don't remember?' he asked.

Not about to strain herself to try, she simply said, 'Not a thing. Want to fill me in?'

'You should… We should… I can't do this lolling on the floor like a pair of teenagers at a make-out party,' Danny mumbled, his arm slowly slipping away from behind her back as he drew himself to his feet.

He held out both hands and she took them despite his last comment, which was currently resonating in the corner of her brain that was in charge of pulse control. Though she knew he hadn't meant anything by it. He never did. That was just Danny. It was habitual for him to keep people tap-dancing and at a distance.

She was pulled to her feet as though she weighed nothing at all, then he slid a warm arm around her waist, the woollen sleeve of his black suit jacket catching against the cotton of her tank top causing it to rub against the sensitive skin of her stomach. She focused on that and not on the immense relief she felt surrounded by all that warmth, strength and the scent of lime.

He let go once he had her seated in a comfortable red leather tub chair. Then, rather than heading around to the comfy-looking swing chair on the other side of his desk, Danny grabbed another guest chair and dragged it over to face hers.

As he sat, she noticed that one side of his dark suit pants was now covered in tiny carpet filaments, hooked evilly into the wool of his trousers. She wondered distractedly if his dry cleaners would have to pull each and every one out with tweezers. If she was female and he smiled when he asked…

He shifted forward, his trousers straining across his solid thighs. Then he took both her hands in his again. Large hands. The hands of a guy who mowed his own lawn. Made his own dinner. Washed his own underwear. They weren't the soft hands of some pampered desk jockey who had someone waiting at home to look after him.

His wide flat thumb pads ran back and forth across the backs of her knuckles. And with each soft, slow, soothing stroke she felt her headache ebb away. Even if the last thing Danny could be accused of being was warm and fuzzy, right now, in that moment, as he held her hands and held her gaze, again she could have sworn she saw quicksilver clouds of concern shoot across his gaze. Something was very wrong here.

'Brooke, do you remember coming to me last week to check on the probate of Cal's will?'

'Yes.' Well, she hadn't remembered, but now she did. Now she only wished she hadn't. Now she wished she'd kept her eyes closed after all. *If wishes were fishes,* as Danny often said. 'And?'

'You fainted because I told you that the reason why none of Calvin's assets have been deferred to you since he died is that he had none. It took an inordinate amount of time for all of his debts to be settled since he lived much of the year overseas. And, once that was done, he was found to be insolvent. Honey, it's all gone. Every last bit.'

And just like that Brooke's wobbly stomach stopped wobbling. Just like that it turned to hot liquid anger. Beautiful, centring, numbing floods of anger.

Danny must have sensed the pulling back, the shutting down, as he squeezed her hands hard. Offering…solace? Understanding? A port in a storm? Whatever he meant by it, that firm touch was all that kept her from throwing up as everything came swimming back to her through the red haze of memory.

All she and Calvin had put in place to make sure she and their young children would be looked after in the event that anything happened to one of them—the house, the life insurance policy, the investments—were gone.

And something had indeed happened. Three months before, instead of coming straight home after winning the Italian Motorcycle Grand Prix, her husband, who happened to be Danny's best friend, had driven a hundred-thousand-dollar Maserati that she hadn't known he'd had off a cliff on the Italian coast with a teenage waif whom she had known about in the passenger seat.

The hot liquid inside of her cooled and solidified into a rod of fortified steel. The wobbles were gone. Her headache was gone. She felt delightfully numb. Except for the gentle strokes infusing life-affirming warmth back into her hands.

She tugged her hands away from Danny's touch, from his sympathy. He linked his long fingers together, sliding them together and apart in a hypnotic rhythm, and within touching distance if she needed them. But she had no intention of giving in to to that kind of comfort. His sympathy made her feel strangely powerless. And right now she needed to be stronger than she'd ever been before.

'Right,' she said, shaking her hair away from her cheeks only to find several pieces stuck there with perspiration. She impatiently pushed them away. 'At this point I will concede that I did in fact faint. I don't think that I would have decided to take a sudden catnap after hearing that.'

The right corner of Danny's mouth jerked, deepening one long heartthrob-grade crease along his right cheek before it thankfully disappeared into a mere memory. 'Brooke, what the hell happened? Where did it all go?'

She gave a small shrug, feeling suddenly as though if she opened her mouth to speak she might instead break down in tears. And tears were not a part of her life any more than fainting was. They were for toddlers with scraped knees, guys who'd had too much to drink and guests on Oprah.

Tears were for people who wanted other people to know about their business.

'What with the sponsorship deals alone he must have made close to three million dollars over the last year,' Danny continued, voicing the words she couldn't find. 'And after house payments, car payments and Beau's school fees, you should still have an excellent nest egg.'

'Don't forget to add agent's fees to the mix of outgoings,' she said pointedly.

Their gazes clashed and held. Hers was red-hot. His was autumn-cool. She could all but see the air shimmer between them. It did that sometimes, as if they were two north poles forced to interact through their connection to Cal, and the laws of nature simply did not approve.

He leant almost imperceptibly backwards, withdrawing from her, emotionally and physically. He held up his hands in surrender, slicing through the shimmering air which went back to normal. 'Don't shoot the messenger, Brooke. Without me he would never have made it out of amateur suburban street racing.'

She sat up straighter. 'Egotistical much?'

'No,' he said, his golden eyes now dark and glinting, 'just honest.'

'Fine,' she shot back, not letting him completely off the hook, for he had been the bastard's best friend. 'If you were God's gift to Cal, then *you* tell me how this happened. As far as I knew, you were looking after that side of things for us.'

Danny blinked, but not quite fast enough that she didn't catch the shadow of surprise that passed behind his glinting gaze.

He crossed his right foot over his left knee, his dark trouser leg straining against might and muscle. And he ran a thoughtful hand over his smooth chin. 'I haven't looked after Cal's finances since he told me that you, in fact, wanted to keep your investments separate from his earnings.'

Brooke's stomach began to curdle. Not as if she was about to pass out again, but deeper than that. As if her whole remembered experience was skew-whiff. As if the people in her life, her support crew, were all on another page from her and had been for years. 'And you didn't think that sounded odd?'

He paused, considering his next words. Then he slowly rested all the way back in his chair. Lounging. Looking as relaxed as if he'd spent the past hour winding down with a glass of his beloved Scotch, not that the two of them were discussing the collapse of her life as she knew it. God, he was too cool. She crossed her arms to stave off a chill.

'I thought that sounded pretty sensible,' he said. 'Diversification is the key to safeguarding your assets. And I thought maybe you wanted to keep some things private.' At that his gaze glanced off hers and out towards the blue horizon glistening back at him from outside his second floor window.

'Me? Keep something private from you?' She bit out a laugh. 'Since Cal's first World Championship I've had a hard enough time keeping the kids' doctor's appointments out of the tabloids. They knew I was pregnant with Lily before I did. But to keep something from you? You have to be kidding.'

His gaze shot back to hers. Though she hadn't a clue what was going on behind those flinty eyes, it didn't stop her from having to bear the full force of his thoughts. Her skin began to both warm and cool under his intense gaze and she took a long slow breath, desperately hoping her reaction wasn't a sign of another fainting spell.

'Danny,' she said, 'you've seen me drunk, hung-over, wretched with the flu. You've seen me with no make-up, in my pyjamas and with my hair full of half-eaten rusk biscuits.

And, no matter how much I've tried to erase the image from my head, you spent one day holding back my hair as I spent two straight hours with my head in the toilet bowl the first day I had morning sickness with Beau.'

Which was more than Calvin had ever done, she thought, using the anger again, feeding off it, wrapping it around herself like a layer of protection as Danny's normally cool eyes were unexpectedly lit warm by the sweep of memories she'd meant to throw his way as some kind of weapon.

'I had forgotten about that,' Danny said, his voice low and intimate. 'Not your most glamorous day.'

'Probably best that you go on forgetting it.'

Danny's cheek twitched again, the right corner of his mouth lifting, creating a hollow in his cheek and a deepening of the beguiling smile line. Unfortunately it was the kind of dimple that could make even the most serious woman forget herself. In her current woolly-headed state, Brooke struggled to keep her focus.

Danny's shoulders moved in a shadow of a shrug. 'Even despite all of those significant moments in our shared history, I would have understood if you had wanted to put some distance between us.'

The thing was, she hadn't seen the need. Ever. So why had Cal? He and Danny had been the closest of friends. If Cal had told him the truth, Danny would fall on Cal's side every time. No matter what. Unless…

'You did know that Cal and I had been estranged for over a year now, did you not?'

She had expected Danny had known about her 'secret' separation from Cal from the moment it had been decided. But when his mouth turned down at the corners, dark storm clouds gathering in his eyes, Brooke realised he truly hadn't had a clue.

'You mean you were planning to divorce?' he asked, his voice so low it created skitters along her arms.

She nodded. Though she felt a sudden unexpected swell of affection for Cal. He'd kept that one promise, giving her time to decide when or whether to share the news with her family and friends before they made any concrete moves away from one another for good.

The swell hit its peak and then sighed away to nothing, like a micron-thin soap bubble. While she'd stayed for Beau and Lily, and she'd tried to seem content, Cal had seen her hesitation to leave him as the chance to systematically cut her legs out from under her.

A great gaping hole took its place in her chest. She wasn't numb any more, or even in pain, just empty. And very alone.

'Nobody had a clue, Brooke,' Danny said. 'I can assure you of that much at least.'

Brooke smiled, but she felt no joy. 'You'd think that was clever. Keeping my cards close to my chest like that. But now the country is mourning one of their most beloved sporting stars. They are raw with it. To them my loss is immediate. But the truth is I lost Cal a long time ago.'

She ran a hand over her eyes. 'And everything I've been trying to avoid is here. Now. Tumbling in on me at a rate of knots.'

Danny didn't say a word. She wondered if he felt some kind of perverse satisfaction in her predicament. He had never been happy that she had married Cal. She had known it from the moment they had first met. He'd never exactly been unfriendly, just reticent. Until over the years they had formed an uneasy truce. A partnership of sorts as cogs in the mighty Calvin Findlay machine.

And now Cal was gone, and her so-called friends—wives

and girlfriends in the racing fraternity—had abandoned her overnight, Danny was right there. Despite their unspoken tensions, he was all she had.

It was time to bring him back to her page.

'What I am trying to tell you,' she said, then took a long deep breath, 'is that I've never kept anything but that from you. It never occurred to me to try. The sad fact of my screwed up, mess of a life is that you, Danny Finch, have been the next best thing to a husband I have known.'

CHAPTER TWO

As soon as those words left her mouth Brooke wished she could take them back.

The next best thing to a husband? What was she thinking? That kind of statement could send the most demonstrative guy into a trembling fit. But untouchable, cool as a cucumber Danny Finch? If only she knew how to make herself faint then she would like to give it a go in that moment!

Instead she stood, ignoring the boneless feeling in her legs, and moved over to the window. She wrapped her arms about her and squinted at the breathtaking view of St Kilda beach. Across the busy road, pristine blue waves lapped peacefully against blindingly bright sand.

'Ignore every word coming from my mouth right now,' she said, rubbing at her temple.

Danny stood too; she could see his reflection in the glass, though he thankfully kept his distance, resting his backside against his desk. 'Don't do it, Brooke.'

'Don't do what?' she asked, her voice rising. 'Panic? Fall apart? You're telling me I am about to lose my home, right? And I don't have enough money to pay Beau's school fees for the last term of the year, even if I decide never to eat again.'

She knew she was being fractious. But his nonchalance in

the face of her meltdown only made her want to shake him, or kick him—anything so that she could get some kind of reaction other than lukewarm tolerance.

Oh, why was she bothering? What were they to each other without Cal anyway? Maybe she should just cut her losses, shake his hand and say, "nice knowing you" and never see him again.

Maybe that was what she should have done. But it had taken more than infidelity and broken promises for her to leave Cal, why should a little embarrassment have her running from the only one left who could shed light on her situation?

'Don't sugar coat it,' she insisted. 'Hit me with it. All of it. I can take it.'

His eyes narrowed. 'It's a little better than you think. You have *exactly* enough to cover Beau's school fees for next term if you decide not to eat ever again.'

She laughed through her nose. 'I take it back. Maybe you could have sprinkled a little artificial sweetener on it.'

She faced him. 'How long do you think it will be before this gets out? Before some reporter follows a trail and finds out that not only was the Father of the Year screwing around, but that he left his kids destitute?'

Danny didn't even flinch at her language; he was used to locker rooms and end-of-season footy trips. She wondered briefly what it would take to crack the façade, what it would take to truly see behind the cool golden gaze.

'Now that the will's out of probate and has been executed it will be filed,' he said. 'It will become public record. So I'd say you have a day if anyone has flagged his name or yours. Maybe two if you're lucky.'

A day? Oh, God. 'But he's been gone for nearly three months,' she said, her voice wavering. 'How can this still be news?'

Danny's fingers dug harder into his arms, pulling at the fabric of his dark suit jacket. And she swallowed down her apprehension, knowing he simply wouldn't know what to do if she suddenly turned into a howling female.

'There's no escaping it, Brooke. You'll be Calvin Findlay's widow until your dying day. Your tombstone will read: *Here lies the wife of the best MotoGP champ this wide brown land has ever seen. May* he *rest in peace.*'

Brooke shot him a wry glare. 'Thanks,' she said, 'that's comforting.'

He shrugged, but he had made her feel better, as his straight talking, no bull attitude often did. He was the one person who didn't make her feel as though he was keeping score. Push and pull. Give and take. With Danny it had never felt like that. With Danny she had always simply felt on the right end of an honest answer, good or bad. And with that she'd felt…safe.

'So now what?' she asked.

'You're going to have to sell the house.' Danny delivered the sucker punch with the same timbre in his voice as he once would have used to thank her for a beautiful dinner party.

'I know,' she said on a resigned sigh.

'And give back the car.'

'Give it to whom?'

Danny's cheek muscle clenched. 'It's leased.'

'Right,' she said, 'of course it is.' Her hands tightened around her elbows and she felt a very little better imagining it was Calvin's neck.

'And you're going to have to get a job.'

She lifted a hand to her eyes and pinched them closed, until she could only see black with swimming patches of colour burned on to her retina from staring too long at the sun-drenched water. 'But Lily's not in school until next year and

I can't leave Beau in care during his upcoming school holidays. Not now.'

Her hand dropped and she shook out her arms to rid them of the pins and needles building within. 'Besides which, the only real job I've ever had was tending bar. And that was ten years ago. Do you know any employer who'd take on anyone with such a sad résumé?'

'I can find work for you here,' Danny said.

She stopped her shaking and blinked to refocus. Of all the things the guy had told her that day, that actually shocked her the most. The Good Sports Agency was Danny's life. His wife, his mistress and his favourite child all rolled into one.

'And what would I do for you, exactly? Upgrade your flights to business class using nothing but my charms? Make your staff boxed lunches? I can do a hell of a Vegemite sandwich. That's about all the practical experience I've had in the last ten years.' She shook her head. 'Thanks, but no. I'm nobody's charity case.'

He raised one dark eyebrow, the cheek crease suddenly getting so close to turning into a full-blown smile that Brooke couldn't drag her eyes away. 'I'm not a charity giver. But I am in dire need of a personal assistant, someone to run interference between my unique receptionist Lucille and my hypersensitive clients. And if I didn't think you would be an asset to my company, I wouldn't have made the suggestion.'

'Yes, but—'

'Yes but nothing. You're a smart woman, Brooke. You're bright. Personable. You have plenty to offer. A prospective employer,' he added after a distinct pause.

And there she'd been thinking for the past eight years that he'd never really warmed to her, that he'd tolerated her for Cal's sake, when all the while he'd thought her…personable. She felt strangely deflated by the bland compliment.

But now was not the time for her to burn bridges. She'd had enough burnt from the other side of the river since Cal's death.

'That's a really generous offer, Danny. I'll think about it. But I can't really make any decisions right this second. Not until I have the kids' needs sorted first.'

Danny nodded. 'Have you got somewhere to stay in the interim? Would your sister take you in?'

Simone. Oh, God. She would have to go through all this again with Simone. Her sister was looking after Lily at work now, and she would have no choice but to fill her in on all the salacious details when she picked her daughter up that afternoon. Her day was getting better and better.

'Not an option,' Brooke said. 'She lives in a one-bedroom apartment with no yard and an unemployed hippy who smokes pot like a chimney. Even if there was room for us, there's no way I'm taking my kids into that kind of atmosphere.'

Danny watched her carefully. Rather than simply taking his aloofness in her stride as she usually did, this time it made her feel flushed and unsettled.

'Well,' she said, masking her sudden sensitivity with brightness, 'since you're in a philanthropic mood, then I absolutely will allow you to let Beau, Lily and me crash on the couch in reception. Sound fair?'

'Problem solved,' Danny said, his lips stretching into an actual smile.

She got a glimpse of neat white teeth and everything. Her heart skipped a beat. Not because that smile meant anything to her personally, but because she was female. And there was simply no denying Danny was gorgeous.

He was urbane, sophisticated and had a sense of humour so sharp it could wound. He was tall, fit and oozed good health. The fact that he was determinedly single meant that he left a path of swooning women in his wake every time he walked out his front door.

Then there was that mouth. Wide, sensuous and kicked up at the corners. And those rare times when he truly smiled? Well, then he was just beautiful. There was no better word to describe him.

It was a great pity then that she had more warmth in her little finger than he seemed to have in his whole body. The guy took cool to a whole new level. And she'd always found it kind of sad. She'd long ago decided it came from being too smart. Too good-looking. Too proud. While having to live out his days amongst mere mortals. *Diddums*.

Brooke cleared her throat of the sudden lump therein. It was past time she left. She'd heard what he had to say, and sitting there sharing a whole range of rare smiles with the guy sure wasn't going to solve any of her troubles.

'One problem. The couch is lumpy,' Danny said. He pushed himself away from the desk and she had to tilt her chin to look up at him.

'The couch?' *The couch?* 'Oh, the reception couch. Bummer.'

'And Lucille is a grub,' he said, the smile still lingering about his eyes. 'She leaves chocolate wrappers all over the place. Greasy, scratchy chocolate wrappers. '

'I like her,' Brooke said, not giving into the strong desire to take a step backwards. 'She's feisty.'

'She's borderline off her nut,' Danny said. 'But she can type like a demon, has better written grammar than even my grand-mother had, and my computer files have never been so orga-nised. If only I could keep her locked to the computer and away from the clients, then my life would be perfect.'

Danny seemed to believe what he was saying, but Brooke

picked up a measure of tenderness, an inadvertent enchantment in his voice. It would be nice for someone to talk that way about her. She almost felt jealous. Of Lucille. Danny's left-of-centre receptionist. She really ought to have just stayed lying down after all.

'So no couch for us, then?' she asked.

He shook his head. Slowly. Left then right. His eyes never leaving hers, his delectable scent drifting past her nose. It really would be more than nice to have someone talk about her, think about her, treat her with even half that much tenderness.

'And I'm sure you'd be much more comfortable staying at my place.'

'Staying?' she repeated, that one word bringing her back from wherever her folly had taken her the past few seconds to real life with such force she dug her toes into the carpet so as not to sway. 'At *your* place?'

He held out both hands, leaving them to hover in the region of her elbows. She must have looked as though she was going to faint again. But she really hoped he wouldn't touch her. She still felt oversensitive and strangely breathless.

'Brooke, this story will get out. The press will hunger for you like never before. You think having them follow you around to see what groceries you like to buy is intrusive? That's nothing compared to how greedy they will be now that the story isn't so rosy. You need somewhere safe to stay until you get on your feet.' He paused, then added, 'And it feels like the least I can do.'

'Danny, I…I don't even know where you live.'

'In the Dandenong Ranges.'

'But that's miles from here,' she shot back.

The dimple returned. She bit her lip.

'Not so many miles. Close enough for me to commute

every day, and far enough that city journos won't be bothered enough to come find you. I have spare cars so you could come and go as you please. And there is plenty of room. Way more than one single guy could ever need. I would be honoured if you looked upon it as a safe haven while you need one.'

It sounded tempting. Too tempting really. Space. Distance. All the while under Danny's far-reaching protection. The kind of protection she would normally eschew, but right now, under these circumstances, after the mess she had landed her kids in, did she have a choice?

'It's a really kind offer. But we'd only be putting you out,' she said half-heartedly.

'You've never put me out.' The certainty in his voice seeped under her skin, warming her from the inside out. 'And it's not my style to make empty gestures, Brooke.'

She dug deep, hoping to find some other option. But there was none. She was the one who had acted like an ostrich for the past several years, head in the sand, pretending she had a blessed life. With her celebrity husband, her huge house in Hawthorn, her beautiful children, her weekly routine of yoga and spa days, she was the envy of every woman who stood reading tabloid magazines in the supermarket. Now those same readers would be licking their chops at the thought that she had just landed flat on her face.

As though he had read her mind, Danny added, 'There's no way in except through a private gate. I am surrounded by forest, and up a mountain. Any press who follow deserve an interview for sheer persistence. And by the time they figure out where you are, and how to climb a tree, this will all be yesterday's news.'

Yesterday's news. Funny, she'd felt like yesterday's news for years now. Ever since the first time she had found another woman's lipstick on Calvin's collar. She wondered when the rest of the country would wake up and realise it too.

'Well, when you put it like that,' she said. 'I accept. Thank you.'

'My pleasure,' he said, bowing from the waist like an old-fashioned gentleman.

He smiled. She smiled back. And then the intercom buzzed, breaking the strange spell that had come over the room. His hand snaked out and pressed a button hidden somewhere on his high-tech desk. 'Lucille,' he said. 'No calls.'

'But it's Gordon Rose. He said you asked him to call.'

He blinked. His eyes growing darker, clouded, as he weighed his options. Should he continue with the troubled widow of his best friend or talk to the highest-paid football coach in the country, the dream catch for any sports agent worth his salt?

Brooke decided to make the easy decision even easier for him. 'You're busy,' she said, backing away and collecting her handbag from a chair near the door.

'Tell him I'll call him back in ten minutes,' Danny said to the disembodied voice of his receptionist, his dark eyes never leaving hers. Then took his finger off the button as Lucille began to protest.

'Danny—' Brooke said.

'He'll keep.' He walked over to join her in the doorway. 'Are you sure you're okay?'

She thought for a second that he might reach out to her again, touch her arm, her waist. To extend some of the tenderness he had shown for his screwball receptionist. Her skin prepared itself, growing taut and tingling. But instead his hands dived into the pockets of his trousers.

One offer of a warm bed and she was thinking their relationship had shifted. He was doing Cal one last favour, by way of her—nothing more. Or perhaps hoping to ease some of his own sense of loss in having Cal's kids around for a couple of weeks. Either way, nothing had shifted.

'No more fainting, I promise,' she said. 'Especially if you're not around to catch me.'

She thought she saw his cheeks go slightly pink. It could have been the reflection from the red feature wall. It must have been. Big, brusque Danny Finch would *never* blush. Any more than she would faint...

Or perhaps he was blushing as he hadn't caught her earlier. She could picture him standing over her, hands deep in his trouser pockets, bemusedly watching her drop, a voice in his head saying, *I'm a busy, important man. Couldn't she have done this on someone else's floor?*

'I'll be in touch,' Danny said, 'regarding when to come pick you guys up. The sooner the better, Brooke.'

She shot him a quick smile, then headed out, down the long hallway littered with glossy photos of sports stars in action and through the empty reception to the lift.

He followed. Ever the gracious host.

The lift doors opened and she stepped inside, alone in the echoing cube, while Danny stood tall and sure on the other side, the king of his domain. She suddenly felt loath to leave him. All that innate confidence was comforting.

The doors started to close. He nodded, his dark eyes sparkling. 'See you soon, Brooke.'

'Bye.'

As the lift took her down to the ground floor, she shook off the layers of emotion wrapped around her. Part despair, part alarm and part unidentified discomfort that she always felt after being in Danny's presence.

He was a tough nut to crack. Some girl some day would break through the shell, but Brooke wasn't entirely sure what they would find beneath. More of the same? Or a deeper reason for his huge ambition and disinclination to settle down? The woman who was able to go there would have to be one in a million. With the patience of a saint and the hide of a rhino.

Some girl. Some day…

Danny stood staring at the silver doors of the lift. His reflection was split right down the middle and all out of kilter, which was exactly how he felt.

He wished Calvin were there with him now. Mostly so he could punch the guy's lights out for what he'd done to Brooke. And then he wanted to drag him up off the floor and deck him again for what he'd done to his own kids.

Cal had never been perfect. Danny knew that. He had been the type of guy who feigned injury during school cricket matches whenever they were behind so he didn't have to play on a losing team. But not looking after his family financially? That was just unforgivable.

Danny ran a hand over his face. What was Brooke to do? He felt for her. Deeply. To the point of actual physical discomfort in his gut. One more reason he felt disturbed.

He'd always admired her, respected her even, for she was a wonderful mum who had all but single-handedly raised two pretty great kids. Coming from a single-parent home himself, he knew how hard that could be. But he'd never been all that sure that he'd *liked* her.

Until that moment when he'd given her the bad news, when her pink cheeks had drained of all colour, when her mouth had gone slack and her willowy body had gone lax, then something inside him had flipped, like a switch turning on a thousand-watt bulb.

Pure instinct had pitched him forward to protect her, to gather her in his arms. An old cricketing knee injury had smarted like hell as he'd held her dead weight, but he had still lowered her to the ground as slowly as he could, her body as delicate and vulnerable as a rag doll. And once he'd let her go, all he'd wanted to do was take hold of her again.

The mere memory of it sent his heart racing. He closed his eyes and remembered her head thrown back, exposing a length of lovely pale neck. Breasts thrust upward. A sliver of tanned skin stretched over her slightly rounded stomach as her tank top separated from the belt line of her beige cargo pants. The feel of skin that had seen a thousand hours at the spa. The smell of her blonde waves tumbling over his arm. Apples and sunshine.

Since the first time he'd met her on that hot May day when Cal had thrown a barbecue party to introduce his friends to his new bride, he'd associated her with apples and sunshine. Apples, sunshine and his best friend.

Danny opened his eyes.

That's Calvin's wife you're thinking that way about, his conscience piped up as he rubbed his hands together, wiping away the tingling sensation in the tips of his thumbs where he had touched her last.

Calvin's widow, actually, his common sense responded. *A woman who is not nearly so invulnerable as she's always had you believe. Not nearly so independent. Not nearly so impervious.*

'Down boy,' Lucille said.

Danny spun to find her sliding back behind her desk with a steaming cup of odd-smelling tea in a mug that read 'World's Best Receptionist'. Needless to say, he had not been the one to buy the mug for her. She'd been a temp a couple of years back. He couldn't actually remember hiring her, but neither had she ever left.

He glared at her. 'Are you talking to me?'

'No need for all that frowning,' Lucille said, before shoving a stick of gum in her mouth, taking a big gulp of tea, then clacking away merrily on her keyboard with fingernails so long he had no idea how she managed to do anything without poking herself. 'I think you're *in* there. And you don't want any more wrinkles. Not unless you're seriously thinking of Botox.'

Danny turned his feet to catch up with his hips. He chose to ignore the Botox comment, though he did rid himself of the frown. 'I'm in *where*, exactly?'

Lucille's frantic fingers stilled. She looked him in the eye, not in the least bit intimidated by his hiring and firing rights. 'Don't look at me like that. I call it like I see it, and that's what you love most about me.'

Danny blinked, not quite knowing where to begin. In the end he went with, 'Are you intimating I don't call it like I see it?'

'Not as often as you like to think you do. See that was me calling it like I see it. Now, tell me exactly how many times you've pictured the blonde up to her neck in hot tub bubbles.'

Danny said nothing, all the while trying to find the words needed to send her out on her ear. But though they gathered in fast abandon beneath his tongue he found he couldn't do it. He thought it his greatest character flaw. 'Think yourself lucky I do hold my tongue at times,' he growled.

Lucille smirked, then went back to her typing.

Danny sauntered over to her desk, wiping a finger across the edge, looking for dust, chocolate crumbs, anything to chide her over, but he found nothing. 'Do you know who that was?'

'Sure,' Lucille said. 'She's that big blond guy's wife. The

motorbike racer who did a *Thelma and Louise* off that cliff in France or wherever with the model. He was splashed all over the magazines a couple of months back. He's been in here once or twice too.' She smiled at him, then typed some more.

'Calvin Findlay,' Danny said, 'was the big blond guy. He won more MotoGP championships than anyone else in history. He won Australian Sportsman of the Year three times.'

'Right,' she said, flicking a handful of multicoloured fingernails in his general direction while still typing with the other hand. 'Him. Was he a client of ours?'

Danny shook his head in amazement. Everyone in Australia knew Calvin Findlay. He'd been a superstar, a classic Aussie bloke. Now of course they would soon know him as a bastard for leaving his family high and dry.

Though he had been in the business long enough to know that none of it would tarnish Cal's image; in fact it would only add to the legend. While poor Brooke would be left behind to deal with the consequences of being cast as the poor deluded wife. It wasn't fair. But then again it had been some time since he'd thought life ever was.

'Why are you still here if you care not a lick about this business?' he asked, his voice gruff.

'I type a million words a minute, make the best cappuccino this side of Lygon Street and your clients are so shocked to see a girl like me here when they get out of the lift they think you're a genius and I am your secret weapon.'

Danny wondered for the umpteenth time what atrocities he had performed in a past life to deserve this woman. 'Are they right?' he asked.

'That you're a genius? Well, of course they are.' Lucille batted her eyelashes and grinned, showing off a decided gap between her large front teeth.

Despite himself, he laughed. He reached down and grabbed a handful from the bowl of M&Ms she always kept on her desk. She tried to slap him but he was too quick.

'So stop yabbering and prove me right,' he said as he walked away.

'Yes, boss,' she called out, and he grinned some more.

Danny retired into his office to try to get some work done and not think about the fact that a single, newly vulnerable, endearingly unsteady Brooke Findlay would be moving in with him.

Showering in his shower.

Sleeping in his house.

Constantly in his line of sight, and thus rarely out of his thoughts, which was where he had purposely tried to keep her for a good eight years.

Nope, he wouldn't think of any of that. Even though he would be spending the rest of the afternoon in his office, which now smelt entirely of apples and sunshine.

CHAPTER THREE

A WEEK later, Brooke stood in the middle of the grand foyer of the beautiful Hawthorn mansion she had called home for the past several years. The house looked so cold now, devoid of furnishings since she had sold or given them away, without scattered toys on the floor, without Beau's bike and dirty shoes resting against the front hall, or scattered feathers from Lily's pink feather boa that she never went anywhere without.

Heavy footsteps drew her from her reverie. She turned with a smile plastered to her face to find Danny coming out of the library with Beau lifted piggyback style.

She blinked, but it didn't change the fact that her serious seven-year-old son, a boy who had long since thought himself too old for such things, had his skinny arms wrapped tight around Danny's neck.

Big, tough Danny Finch. A man who'd bowled his last representative cricket match with a broken finger. A man so unforgiving he'd had Australia's top football commentator sacked for making disparaging and untrue remarks about one of his clients. Which was why the endearing image of his large hand resting so gently over her son's small one was so hard to digest.

The second Lily tumbled into the room, her dilapidated

feather boa wrapped about her shoulders, curls galore escaping from her blonde pigtails, twirling with her arms held wide, loving all the extra space, clueless as to what it meant, Brooke turned away from Danny and Beau before they could see the hazardous emotion building inside her.

'Okay, guys,' Brooke said, her voice stronger than she felt. 'Beau and Danny have checked that everything is switched off, the doors are all locked, the windows are all shut, right?'

She glanced briefly at Danny, who smiled his assent.

'Great. So are we all ready?'

'Ready!' Lily shouted.

'Beau, honey? All set?'

Beau nodded.

'That just leaves you,' Danny said.

'Everything's ticked on my list,' she said, but she could see in his eyes that he was after more from her.

It shouldn't have felt so novel, him being there for her. He'd been there for her numerous times through the years. Checking up on her when Cal had been out of town. She'd always thought he'd been doing so at Cal's insistence. It had been an insurance policy that had told her how much Cal really cared despite his other failings. But the now unmistakable level of attention in Danny's gaze had her questioning even that small satisfaction.

But now wasn't the time for all that. Beau was waiting for her with that serious patience he always exuded. Lily gave up twirling and moved in to take her by the hand, looking up at her with big expectant eyes. And Danny watched her as though he was ready in case she stumbled. He would not let her fall. Lucky her.

She ran a hand over her daughter's hair. 'I'm more than ready. I'm excited. A new home. A new school. A new start.

It's like the beginning of a movie when the credits roll and you feel all excited because anything could happen next. Don't you think?'

'But my bed's gone,' Lily said. 'Where am I going to sleep?'

'Are we going to Auntie Simone's?' Beau asked.

'No, honey,' she said. 'Auntie Simone only has one bedroom and that's where she sleeps. And since you guys are so used to having your own bedrooms, she thought it wasn't fair to ask the three of us to share a couch.'

'Eeeuw,' Lily said, scrunching her face up.

Brooke gathered Lily in, crossing her wrists in front of her little girl's neck, holding on tight. Lily tipped her head back and grinned. Brooke leaned down and kissed her daughter's forehead. 'My sweet kiddlywinks, we are going on a car trip into the mountains and there we'll stay in Danny's house in the rainforest.'

'Will Dad know where we are?' Lily asked, her sweet face the picture of innocence.

Brooke swallowed down the lump in her throat that always came with such conversations. Her kids were so so young. It took some kind of fancy footwork to get them to understand what had happened to their dad without scaring them, or telling them more than they needed to know at the ages of seven and four. 'Of course he will. Haven't I told you he can see everything from heaven?'

'That's right,' Lily said, satisfied.

Though Brooke wondered if down below had as good a view.

She winked at Beau and gave him a big smile. His cheek twitched and he sniffed and pushed his Harry Potter glasses higher on his nose. If she wasn't careful he would turn into another Danny, with everything hidden behind a perfect mask.

She'd have to spend some one-on-one time with her little

boy the first minute she could. But for now she shifted Lily behind her and leaned in and gave her son a big kiss on the cheek. He didn't turn away and cry foul as he usually did when she kissed him in public; he just took it. And that more than anything showed her how anxious he really was.

'You are such a brave boy,' she whispered, pulling back to shine every ounce of love she had for him through her eyes.

He gave her a watery smile and she took it. Treasured it. Hugged it tight to herself.

When she pulled away she found herself caught up in a cloud of Danny's aftershave. Tangy, citrus, drinkable. She had the funny feeling she would for evermore identify that scent with him. The scent that had the same effect on her as smelling salts. Every time she encountered it her senses stretched, as though rousing her from a long slumber.

Before she could talk herself out of it she leaned in and gave him a small kiss on the cheek too, her lips rasping against stubble. That mixed with his scent and the rewarding feel of his strong bicep brushing ever so slightly against her chest only told her how very very long it had been since she had been this close to a man. Weeks. Months. Years. Forever.

Pathetically long, especially for a woman who until recently had been married. And that had to be why she was still leaning into the guy and paying close attention to his much-lauded attributes.

She pulled back, her eyes taking a moment to refocus to find he was looking at her as though he knew exactly what had been going through her head.

Too smart. Too good-looking. Too proud, she reminded herself before moving straight on through to *Stupid! You're looking a gift horse in the mouth and doing your best to find*

*a way to screw it up. And that isn't an option when you've got
two very important young people relying on you to make the
right choices. All the right choices.*

She nodded, once, in thanks. And he nodded back, his lips
curving back into a small smile, which made itself felt as a
warm ache deep within her.

'Right,' she said, backing far enough away so that she no
longer felt wrapped up in his scent and heat and remarkable
gravitational pull. 'Let's do this thing.'

She took one last look around the empty foyer of their
grand house—a place she had worked very hard to make into
a home for her atypical family—the only home Beau and
Lily had ever known. She could already feel herself discon-
necting from the house, as though its soul had already
moved on and she was the only one still lingering, hanging
on too tight.

She hitched her handbag onto her shoulder, tucked Lily's
sticky hand in hers, walked to the front door and opened it to
find a throng of press waiting outside. The word had spread
that she was on the move and why. She was fresh meat for the
carnivores. The woman scorned. The perfect life shattered.
The tall poppy cut down in full flower.

'Mummy?' Lily said, her voice wavering as she slid to hide
behind Brooke's legs.

Brooke lifted her daughter onto her hip until she could feel
her fine blonde curls sliding against the bottom of her chin,
her blood pumping too fast through her veins.

'It'll be okay, baby,' she whispered, trying to convince
herself as much as her daughter, 'I promise.'

And then, just as she had decided to slam the door and stay
in the house until the bank sent people to drag her out, she
felt Danny move up behind her.

Warm and tall and broad and strong. Calvin's right-hand man. Her silent protector. And if she was very good and very careful he might just remain that way for a long while yet.

'It's okay, Brooke,' Danny said when she took the first step, his deep voice giving her something sure to concentrate on. 'I've done this a thousand times before. It looks scarier than it is. You'll be fine.'

She had to bite back a desire to scream at everyone to get the hell back, knowing it would only frighten Lily all the more. 'Keep talking,' she begged.

'See the black Jag on the kerb?'

She nodded.

'That's your target,' he said. 'Don't look left or right. Don't listen to a word they say. Just keep your chin level with the ground, put one foot in front of the other and head to the car. Now, let's go.'

He tucked his fingers into the rear belt loop of her cargo pants. She covered his hand, curling her fingers around his and holding on for dear life. And then she pushed through, with Danny's car parked on the street at the end of the driveway her holy grail.

'Did you know about Felice?' one reporter asked.

'Ignore them,' Danny said, so close behind her his toes jutted up against the backs of her shoes.

'Is it true Calvin pissed it all away?' asked another journo.

'They're only trying to get a rise out of you,' Danny said, giving her a small twist to the left to avoid a camera bag she was about to trip over.

'Was Calvin even the kids' real father?' yet another reporter spat at her.

At that one Brooke's head jolted to the right. Making jabs at Calvin was one thing. Gossiping about her had become a national pastime. But if anyone even dared to say, much less *think*, anything that would affect her kids…

She frantically searched the sea of sweaty faces to find the culprit, but through her furious gaze they were all a blur.

Danny's hand slid from her belt loop to glide around her waist, his long fingers gripping her hip. His little finger dipped between her cargo pants and her skin. She knew that last part was accidental but it was enough to draw her focus away from the crowd.

'Don't even think about it, Brooke. Just keep moving forward. Now,' he insisted, his voice so relentless against her ear she managed to pull herself one step back from rabid to do what he said.

She tugged Lily closer and picked up her pace again, managing to kick a couple of random shins on her way through, which made her feel a little better.

The car doors unlocked as Danny clicked the remote, then the back door was magically open, his hand was gone from her and Lily was hauled out of her arms and inside the low-slung car in three seconds flat.

Once she saw her kids were safe, she hit the front seat running, amazed that Danny had managed to distribute them with care when if it had been her alone, under the same duress, the same press of bodies, she would have likely thrown them in and herself after them.

Danny folded his long legs into the driver's seat and gunned the engine, slinking out into the street in his big quiet car, and then they were away. The whole thing couldn't have lasted longer than thirty seconds, but Brooke was breathing as if she had run a marathon.

She twisted in her seat and fussed over the kids, making sure they were buckled in. Soon enough Beau's portable

PlayStation pinged and Lily made it her mission to count the number of green cars she saw along the way, and, just like that, the kids were happy just being kids.

Brooke turned back to the front, did up her seat belt and breathed out a shaky breath. And then she began to tremble. She wrapped her arms tight about herself.

'You warm enough?' Danny asked, flicking a glance her way and playing with the temperature controls.

'I'm fine,' she said, but her unsteady voice gave her away. She managed a small laugh. 'As good as can be expected.'

He glanced at her again, as long as he safely could with his eyes off the road. Again she was taken aback by the rich sentiment in his eyes. That was almost as unsettling as running the gauntlet had been.

'Just get us out of here,' she said, and turned away from his heady gaze to watch the suburbs pass by in a blur.

The tight tram-clogged streets of Melbourne's eastern suburbs transformed into wide, gently undulating main roads which then gave way to tight streaks of dusty bitumen curling ever upwards into the Dandenong Ranges.

Tall, thin, dark-green trees towered over the road, sending cool flickering shadows over the car. Brooke's breath made small patches of white on the car window. It reminded her of family trips to Sorrento years before when she and Simone had written rude messages about one another within the fog.

'You're very quiet over there,' Danny said, the first words spoken by either of them in half an hour.

Brooke tilted her head away from the window. 'Sorry, I was a million miles away and twenty-odd years ago.'

'No need to apologise. I'm used to having only my own company driving up here. It's nice to have someone else in the car.' He shot her a brief smile.

'Even if that person hasn't given you anything by way of enlightening conversation?'

His smile broadened. 'Even so.'

She pulled herself upright and made to check over her shoulder when Danny said, 'They're both asleep. Have been since the first moment we could see the mountains.'

Brooke checked anyway. Beau was curled up in a neat little ball, while Lily was splayed out, spreadeagled, mouth open. Her heart eased.

When she looked back, Danny was staring at her forehead, his face creased into a full-on grin.

'What?' she said, looking up, but all she could see was the edge of her brow.

'You've got a glaring red spot on your forehead from leaning on the window.'

Brooke spun back to the window, trying to measure her reflection. She reached up to rub at the hot spot, but her hand hovered then dropped away. Her hair was a mess and full of dust. She had dark rings under her eyes. A red lump on her forehead wasn't going to do any more damage than was already there. 'I'm broke. Alone. And now I look like a bag lady. Here's to new beginnings!'

Danny watched her in the side reflection. His smile eased, though his eyes remained crinkled in amusement. 'You're not alone, Brooke.'

Something in his voice had her turning back, but he was already looking to the front. His smooth jaw relaxed. His right elbow resting on the windowsill, only the tips of the fingers of his right hand resting on the steering wheel while the left hand did all the work. Once again his lovely hands caught her attention. Enough that she felt the need to stop looking at them.

'I notice you didn't tell me that I don't look like a bag lady,' she said.

His dimple deepened. Was staring at his dimple, being re-assured by his dimple, getting prickly feelings skittering across the back of her neck at the sight of his dimple any better than feeling the same way about his large, sure hands. Or worse? She turned and faced dead front, keeping her eyes on the road with as much focus as if she was the one driving.

'You are a bit dishevelled perhaps, but certainly nothing like any bag lady I've ever seen,' Danny said. Then, after a pause, 'I didn't realise you were fishing for compliments or I would have said something sooner. Excuse my manners.'

'I wasn't! I… Oh, shut up.'

Brooke saw the gleam return to his eyes and gave in. She couldn't win this argument. Not while she was still feeling wobbly in the knees after her encounter with the press. Give her a hot bath, half an hour with her yoga mat and a glass of white wine and then she would gladly take him on.

Soon the car slowed and turned left. Danny eased up a skinny winding gravel road surrounded on both sides by towering shadowy forest. Bright sunlight and shadows dappled over her skin, causing her to squint through the thick woods to make out what they were heading towards.

'Is this a private road?' she asked. 'It could do with some council attention. If anybody comes the other way, you're both stuck.'

'That won't be a problem. This is my driveway,' Danny said.

'Oh.' *Oh, indeed.*

Once Brooke was sure they couldn't go much higher, the forest suddenly cleared, leaving great shafts of sunshine to slice down upon the most amazing house she had ever seen.

A great irregular multi-level home rambled down the side

of the steep cliff face. Masses of wide, high windows, jutting balconies and an eclectic mix of burnt-umber wood panels, muddy cream shingles and pale-coffee-coloured brick covered in twisting green ivy gave the structure the appearance of having grown out of the forest.

They pulled up in front of a five car garage with a matching shingled roof, but Danny just parked the car out front. The hum of the engine and the air-conditioning faded to a strange kind of quiet.

No press. No radio. No white noise. Just the soft whisper of a light wind sighing through a million leaves. It was so hushed Brooke could actually hear herself think. Which maybe wasn't such a good thing.

She opened the car door, stretching out her stiff limbs, feeling as if they had driven five hundred kilometres, not fifty. The kids were out of the car and running, exploring, before her flat canvas shoes hit the golden gravel of the neatly swept driveway. A pristine green, rock-bordered lawn extended from the edges of the gently curving path, eventually melding into lush palms and mossy undergrowth. It looked like something out of a children's novel. If fairies made their homes between the rocks and trees she would not have been all that surprised.

A jingle of keys and a tangy scent far cooler than the shady forest about them brought her back to the present. Danny ambled to lean against the side of the car next to her.

'It's quite something, don't you think?' he asked, squinting to fend off the burn of reflected sunlight from the vast, arched curtain-free window on the very top floor. Somehow she just knew that behind the stunning window lay his bedroom.

'It's something all right.' She faced him. 'How is it that I have never been here before? How is it that I had no idea you lived in a place like this? How is it that I always pictured you living in some slick black and silver bachelor pad on the top floor of some building in town?'

He held up a hand to shield his face, then turned a pair of dark bronze eyes her way. 'You tell me.'

Brooke looked away, pretending to be focused on her kids, but Danny knew better. He also knew the answer to her questions.

She'd never before been here because this place was his retreat. His haven of peace and quiet. And for him to have invited *anybody* here—for dinner, for a game of tennis, to stay over—that took some leap of faith on his part. And she had pictured him living in some steel skyscraper because she had never been interested enough to find out the truth.

But the funny thing? The kicker? That day in his office a week before, it had occurred to him that over the years he had never bothered to find out all that much more about her either. And that day, and every day since, it had felt like some kind of vital imperative that now he find out what that more was.

'Puppy!' Lily called out as a galumphing streak of dark fur bolted from the side of the house.

His chocolate Labrador sprinted around the car and then screeched to a dusty halt at his feet. The dog's whole body shook with glee, but he knew better than to jump up. Not after the number of black suits Danny had gone through those first weeks…

'You have a dog,' Brooke said.

'I have a dog,' Danny said, crouching down to rub the Lab behind its soft floppy ears.

'Since when?'

'Since about two years ago. It's the longest live-in relation-ship I've had since I moved out of home. It has been a steep learning curve.' He reached down and scratched the dog behind the ears and earned a thumping back leg for his efforts.

'Tell me about it,' Brooke said, squinting suspiciously at the dog as though he was the one who'd cheated on her.

'What's her name?' Lily asked as she trundled back to the car, huffing and puffing.

'*His* name is Buckley. He's named after Nathan Buckley, of Collingwood, the greatest football player this sports fan has ever seen.'

Lily screwed up her nose. 'Football? I hate football.' But then she leaned in for a great big hug, grabbing huge hunks of fur as she did so.

Danny laughed. His dog hadn't had much experience with sticky-fingered kids, but Buckley seemed to be handling it with much aplomb, his pink tongue lolling out of his mouth as he leaned into the small blonde. Danny felt a shot of pride that he'd brought the creature up so well.

'And how did I not know you had a dog?' Brooke asked, her voice accusing. 'We discussed getting one for the kids only six months ago and you never once even mentioned…this.'

'Consider yourself told.'

'But—'

'Don't sweat it,' he said, his voice humming with laughter at her comical expression. 'What's past is past. New beginnings, remember?'

Her frowning gaze moved from the dog and back to him. He figured she was thinking that a lot of things were past, and now that Cal was gone they probably ought to have slowly but surely drifted out of one another's lives.

But, as the two of them stood there adding new layers to their impressions of one another, he would have put money on the fact that they wouldn't be drifting any time soon.

CHAPTER FOUR

'LET'S head inside, guys,' Danny said.

'Can Buckley come too?' Lily asked.

'Of course. Inside!' Danny called out. He clicked his fingers and Buckley turned on a dime and bolted around the side of the house. Lily followed, her pink sneakers kicking up mounds of dry dust. Soon a vague faraway flapping of a doggy door split the air and then a few moments later it flapped again.

'Did what I think happened just happen?' Danny asked.

'Yep,' Brooke said, her frown dissolving. 'And you'd better get used to it. That one's impossible. Unexpected. And uncontrollable by man or beast.'

Much like her mother, he thought. 'I'm suddenly having second thoughts. Can I rescind the invitation?'

Brooke turned a smile his way. Her big green eyes shining, her cheeks pink from the touch of the sun during the drive, her lips stretched wide and glossy and smooth. His chest tightened, the muscles clenching as though he'd lifted a heavy weight. For the first time ever he actually wished Lucille was there to put him in his place as in that moment he needed it.

'It's far too late for that,' Brooke said. 'Now that Lily and Buckley have met, we might never be able to get them apart.'

She tucked Beau under her arm, wrapping him in a one-armed embrace, and headed towards the front door, her blonde hair swinging, her tanned calves contracting with each step, her supple body swaying in a purely feminine manner with no effort or purpose.

Impossible, Danny thought. *Unexpected. And uncontrollable?* That was some combination. He cleared his throat, shoved that wayward thought deep down inside and jogged to catch up.

When he unlocked the front door Beau twisted out of Brooke's grip and ran through the house to find Lily and Buckley. Danny threw his keys into a bowl on the front hall table and then quietly followed Brooke as she took the tour.

Her head tipped back as she looked up into the thirty-foot ceiling of the curious three-storey, oval-shaped foyer. Her eyes grew wide with wonder as she discovered the sunken den, the raised kitchen and the S-shaped swimming pool curling around the side of his house. Her mouth hung open as she traversed the library loft at the top of a skinny curling staircase.

He took immense pleasure in her unsophisticated wonder. It was one of her most endearing traits—her capacity to be constantly surprised, no matter what life threw at her. Did that make her naïve? Maybe. But, watching her in that moment, he only wished he had a tenth of her naïvety.

'Danny,' she said, turning to him with an accusatory tone. 'This place is amazing. Did you find it? Or build it? Or did you wave a magic wand?'

'I bought it about six years ago. The wife of one of my clients is a real estate agent. I told her I was looking for something unique, private, a home I would never want to leave, and when this came up she thought of me.'

'A place you would never want to leave? That's pretty romantic.'

'More reactive than romantic, I'm afraid. I moved around a lot as a kid,' he said. From one tiny, airless, windowless council flat to another, every time his mother needed a fresh start after another failed relationship that sent her spiralling backwards, he didn't feel the need to add.

Brooke smiled, her eyes filled with awe, and he was infinitely glad he hadn't soured her mood with a dose of reality.

'It's gorgeous,' she said. 'Like something out of a fairy tale. I always thought our place was too big for one small family. I never quite knew what to do with half the rooms. But this...'

This was why he'd never brought anybody here. He knew it was ostentatious. Hell, that was what he'd loved about the place. The pure fantasy element. His castle in the clouds. Okay, so maybe he'd held on to a tiny bit of wonder all these years.

He cleared his throat and explained, 'I worked bloody hard to get where I am today and this is my compensation.'

'Amen to that,' she said. Then she unexpectedly threaded her hand through his arm and gave it a light squeeze. She was close enough that he could smell her hair, the heat from the car bringing out the apple scent. She shot him one last glance, half encouraging, half puzzled, and then let go, sliding her fingers free, so that she could continue her tour through the lower floor.

He stood his ground, for suddenly he couldn't move a muscle. Something strange was going on. Every touch, every flicker of her soft eyes, every change of shape of her soft lips seemed to take on a new significance to him. A new magnitude. A new kind of brilliance.

But she was just a woman. In an old tank top, loose knee-length cargo pants and canvas shoes, not some kind of goddess. And she was his best friend's wife. No matter what else might have changed, she would always be that. Even though he was pissed off with Cal, he still owed it to the code of mateship to keep that very much in mind.

'What DVDs do you have?' Beau asked, emerging into the foyer from the doorway that led to the billiard room.

Brooke followed in his wake and ran a hand over his soft dark hair. 'Beau,' she chastised gently.

Danny sent Brooke a quick smile to tell her it was okay. 'What sort of movies do you like?'

Beau shrugged and moved slightly further into his mother's protection. 'I like ones with lots of cops and shootings and stuff.'

'Beau!' Brooke said again. 'He's pulling your leg, Danny. He isn't allowed to watch movies with cops or shootings or especially *stuff.*'

'No problem,' Danny said, poking out his bottom lip and nodding as if he wasn't all that fond of such movies anyway. Though, being a red-blooded male, the bulk of his DVD collection was made up of exactly that type of film. 'Though that only leaves us soppy chick stuff or…*The Lion King.*'

Beau's eyes widened, before settling back into a vision of boredom. 'I guess that would be okay.'

'Done. How about you take Lily into the den and pick out a good seat for you both and I'll set it up.'

'Which one's the den?'

Danny flicked a glance across the foyer and through to the other side of the house. 'The room with the video projector.'

Beau's feigned boredom disappeared as his bright blue eyes skittered in the direction of such a room as though drawn by a magnet.

'Go on,' Danny said.

Beau didn't need to be told three times, he uncurled himself from Brooke's embrace and ran off, calling out, 'Come on Lily! Last one there gets a snake bite.'

'Not fair!' Lily called out from somewhere deep inside the house before she came clamouring by.

Brooke felt a strange new kind of tension as her kids bundled excitedly inside the far room, leaving her alone with Danny. Probably because things were going far too easily. She reminded herself this wasn't a holiday and to be prepared for the moment reality came flooding back in.

'Good move,' she said. '*The Lion King* is his favourite movie, you know.'

Danny smiled. In fact he looked pretty pleased with himself. 'I knew that, actually.'

'And when, pray tell, did you purchase said DVD?'

Danny's smug grin diminished, his eyes narrowed, and he didn't answer.

'Before or after I agreed to stay here?' she asked.

His gaze darkened, becoming unreadable. Pure Danny. 'Around about that time.'

She crossed her arms, mostly to protect herself against the goose bumps that sprung up all over her skin when he looked at her that way, which was odd as he had looked at her that way a thousand times before and she'd always just brushed it off. 'That predictable, am I?'

'Just predictable enough,' he said, before winking and smiling so that his dimple came out to play, then he sauntered towards the den.

Brooke stayed right where she was for several gob-smacked moments. Had he really just winked at her? Cool, aloof, debonair Danny Finch?

Well, she for one felt not in the least bit cool. She actually felt a fair bit flustered. Her blood rushed so close to the surface of her skin it tingled. From the effect of one quick, so brief it could have all been in her imagination, wink.

So she needed a hot bath, half an hour with her yoga mat, a glass of white wine *and* a good shrink. Though the shrink would just say that her atypical reactions were the product of depleted confidence and she couldn't trust her own decisions since her mojo—that special something that made her her—was on the fritz. She hoped it was only temporary. She hoped that a few days out of the public eye to get her affairs in order would bring her mojo back. Because the lack thereof was beginning to show itself in weird and not so wonderful ways.

Placing one foot in front of the other to get herself moving in the right direction, she found the den, a long, high-ceilinged, sunken room with row upon row of DVDs lining the near wall. A dark masculine lounge suite and a bar took up the far end of the room, while in front of her a group of chairs arced around a massive projector screen.

Beau was seated in the prime position, right in front. She had half expected him to have settled Lily in a spot in which her back was to the screen, but she was instead squished in next to him. In the same one-seater chair.

Brooke stopped in the doorway, her hand to her heart. For all the bluster and attitude and stiff upper lip, Beau was just a little kid trying to cope the best way he knew how. And that meant being the grown-up, looking out for his little sister.

Just like Simone had done for her years before. Though Simone had been eighteen, she had been thirteen and they'd lost their parents in one hit. Still Beau was seven and sensitive and trying to act the man in the family now he was the only one left.

'Where should I sit, Beau?' she asked from the doorway, letting him continue to have some control.

He shrugged. 'We're fine. You can go unpack or whatever.'

'Yeah, Mum. You can go,' Lily said, shifting so that she could lean her head on her brother's shoulder since he for once was letting her do so. Two little souls snuggled together in the semi-darkness; she was so grateful that they had each other. There was a connection, an understanding, a bond they had in losing their father. A bond she would never share.

'You sure you want to watch this on your own?' she asked, the lump in her throat so large she could barely get the words out. 'It gets pretty scary with Scar and the hyenas.'

'It's not that scary,' Beau said. 'I've seen scarier.'

Danny stood in front of the entertainment unit, flicking the DVD case from one hand to the other. Watching her, waiting to see if she might change her mind, but she just gave him one brief nod.

He put the DVD into the machine. 'Well, buddy,' he said, 'you're a braver man than me.'

Danny gave the kids a comforting smile and then slid around the chairs, moved past Brooke and behind her as the room lit up with music and colour.

'So what's your next trick?' she murmured to keep her voice under the sound of the opening scene.

'Next trick?' he asked, his voice tickling against the back of her hair.

'The movie lasts less than two hours. So what then?'

'I thought I was a bit brilliant with that one idea and didn't think past it to another one. Now you've made me feel like a one trick pony.'

She laughed, the gentle feeling easing some of the ache in her heart. 'You'll get over it, Danny, I have no doubt.'

'I don't know. I'm an ideas man by trade. And now you've made me question my very self-belief.'

Brooke turned her head, just enough so that she could see his elegant profile. 'Danny, it would take a nuclear bomb to shift your self-belief.'

He smiled down at her. A smile of warmth and understanding. But behind the smile was something else. Something he was holding back.

In a burst of pure feminine intuition, she knew that just standing by her wasn't enough for him. He wanted to reach out and touch her. His restraint was palpable, and so tightly sprung she could as good as feel him reaching his arms around her, tucking them along her stomach. She could picture resting her arms atop his, and leaning back against him.

While her kids gave one another solace, it would feel good to be that close to someone too. Who was she kidding? It would feel good to be that close to Danny. To lose herself in his rock-solid build. Oblivion for a few sweet moments. To remind herself that she was still alive. And vital. And not alone.

But that was just ridiculous. She and Danny didn't even like each other all that much. They had put up with one another for Cal. And now Cal was gone, it didn't take a genius to figure out they were using one another for a last little bit of a link to the husband and friend they had lost.

When this had all blown over, when she'd found her feet and had a job, and a place to live, then this feeling, this need, would all fast become a memory. And their acquaintance would fade.

Then there would no longer be a handyman on tap when she found a dead snake in her pool. No guy who actually meant it when he offered to help with the washing-up after a dinner party. No guy showing up to watch Beau's school cricket matches. No more late-night phone calls pretending he had a pertinent question when all the while he was simply checking up on her.

Suddenly Buckley snuffled between them, pressing Brooke forwards and Danny backwards before slobbering all over Brooke's hand. Then he tumbled into the den.

'Buckley!' Lily called out.

'Shh,' Beau said, though he pulled on Buckley's collar until he was sitting up between the two of them, their small hands buried in the fur at his back as he panted and revelled in their attention.

And thankfully the enchanted fog that had come over Brooke was broken. She cleared her throat and turned away from the doorway, slipping past Danny, purposely ignoring his scent, and his large warm body, and the sense that he wanted to hold her.

'Do you mind if I make a phone call? After I wash my hands,' she said, looking at imaginary slobber remains beneath her fingernails. 'I'd like to let my sister know where we are.'

'Of course,' he said, his voice a rumbling whisper. 'You don't have to ask. For as long as you stay, this is your home. Treat it as such.'

Brooke glanced up. 'It's a nice sentiment, Danny, but I can't see myself traipsing around the kitchen in my underwear any time soon.'

Okay, so that was nerves talking, for she suddenly did feel unbelievably nervous. Blame it on the stifling tension that had sprung up from nowhere. But it hadn't sprung up from nowhere. Not really. It had always been there between them. They'd just never been in a situation where they'd had the chance to really notice it, or to think about what it meant.

'It would probably be for the best if you dressed for breakfast,' he drawled. 'And I'll endeavour to do the same.' His eyes remained on hers but her skin warmed as though he had given her a lazy once-over.

'Right you are,' she said, nodding as though they were dis-cussing the house rules for replacing empty milk cartons rather than their collective state of undress. All the while she fought to wipe away the image of Danny wandering into the kitchen in nothing bar tight black underpants looking like some kind of god. Because they would be black. And beneath his clothes he would surely be godlike…

'Ah, the phone?' she said, pointing over her shoulder and taking three steps back.

'There are several. The closest is in the kitchen and it's a portable.' He swept an arm in front of him.

She gave him a tight-lipped smile and hotfooted it to the kitchen, where she found a neat black phone on the kitchen bench beside a wrought iron fruit bowl filled with mail and no fruit.

'Is it a local call from here to Melbourne?' she asked before dialling.

Danny leant a hip against the bench, picked up the mail and began flicking through it, but his eyes remained on hers. Eyes the colour of molten bronze and fuelled by such potent charisma she couldn't deny the skittish waves in her chest. 'What did I just say?' he asked.

Not a thing about black underpants, Brooke thought. 'Um, treat this like it's my own home?'

'That's right.' He tore one letter open, glanced at the contents, then screwed it up and tossed it towards a stainless steal bin in the corner. It landed dead centre with a soft swoosh.

'Skilful,' she said.

'You have no idea.'

Brooke blinked and tried to remember what she was doing in the kitchen.

Thankfully Danny turned away. He opened the fridge and

stared at the contents for a good half minute. Such a guy thing. Cal used to do it all the time. Wasting electricity. Letting out all the cold air. When he had no idea what he was looking for. It used to drive her crazy!

But this *wasn't* her home. It was his. And she was a guest. A very grateful guest who had to call her only sibling to explain why she had chosen to stay with Danny rather than with her.

So Brooke took herself and her insubordinate nasal glands outside and far *far* away from the heady scent of citrus. She chose a park bench in Danny's side yard and sat. She glanced up to see if Danny was watching her but the huge kitchen windows reflected only the rainforest and pool fence behind her.

She took a deep breath and called her sister's direct line at her city law office.

'Simone Morgan,' her sister's voice cut through the ring tone in a blistering rush.

'Simone, it's Brooke.'

'Well, well, well, if it isn't my own celebrity sister. Saw you on the news just now.'

Brooke could all but see her sister leaning back in her big office chair, sliding off her shoes and placing her feet on the corner of the desk. Brooke rubbed at her temples with her forefinger and thumb. 'Must be a slow news day if a woman moving house is newsworthy.'

'The slowest,' Simone agreed. 'Now, my little friend, was that strapping Danny Finch I saw tucked in behind you all snug and cosy and driving you away in his nice big car?'

'It was.' *Here goes...* 'We are staying with him for a while. Until things cool down.'

Simone's silence was deafening.

'I didn't ask you,' Brooke said, 'because you don't have the room for all three of us. I didn't want to be underfoot. And you know I love Jerry but I can't ask him to smoke outside in his own home. And we couldn't afford a hotel, and Danny was good enough to offer, so—'

'Hey, honey, you don't have to convince me. You know what I think of your Danny.'

'He's not my Danny,' Brooke grumbled, hoping against hope Simone wouldn't start in on all that again. For years Simone had had a ridiculous theory that the reason Danny hadn't settled down was because he had some kind of big boy crush on her. Not that he was stubborn, and superior, and left the fridge door open far too long and was just too much damned hard work for any sensible woman to take on.

Brooke knew the only reason Simone had kept on with it was because it got under her skin. And there was nothing her big sister enjoyed more.

'Fine,' Simone said. 'I shall zip my big mouth shut. So how long is this little arrangement going to last? forever and ever? Oops, there I am, not shutting up.'

Brooke ignored her and kept to message. 'The kids would love to see you soon, though. If you have a day free this weekend I could bring them around. Or meet you at the zoo. Or they love that St Kilda place on the beach you took them to for the weekend last year. Or something…'

'I'll let you know later in the week, okay?' Simone said. 'We have a huge defamation case we are defending this week. If it finishes early I'll let you know. Give me Danny's phone number again. Just in case.'

Brooke did as she was asked. Then said, 'Talk to you tomorrow?' even though it was rhetorical.

'Sure. See ya.' And Simone hung up.

Brooke lowered the phone to her lap. Her palms were sweating. Her pulse rate as high as if she'd jogged around the house. She was twenty-seven years old, had lived away from home since she was eighteen, had been married since she was nineteen, had been a mother herself since she was twenty, and her big sister still made her feel like a burdensome brat. Push and pull. Give and take. The pressure was suffocating.

She took a few moments to pull herself together before heading back inside to find Danny with his head still in the fridge. It upset her more than it ought to have that he was acting so like Cal.

'Everything okay?' he asked, coming out of the fridge with nothing.

'Fabulous.'

'Anyone else you need to call?'

She shrugged. 'I have no one else.'

'That's a bit dramatic.'

'Dramatic?' She slowly placed the phone back into its cradle. 'Should I give a quick buzz to any of the other MotoGP wives who dropped me like a hot potato? Or perhaps one of the other mums at Beau's school who whispered behind their hands whenever we walked by after Cal died? I'm sorry, Danny, but I've come to realise that by and large people suck and I don't owe them a damn thing.'

Okay, so she was feeling a little dramatic. But first there was Simone, then the flashbacks associated with the open fridge, and being caught up in Danny's compelling gaze made her feel claustrophobic. And, like a trapped wildcat, she was bound to lash out.

Danny slowly came around to her side of the bench. His citrus scent was stronger than usual, chilled as it was by the cool of the fridge. 'I would hate to be on your bad side, my friend,' he said.

'So don't be,' she shot back.

'Never will be,' he promised, not missing a beat.

She glanced up to find him looking down at her, his expression dead serious. He only looked away to pull up a kitchen stool, then sat down.

Don't kid yourself, her subconscious up and said as she slowly sank on to the seat next to his. *This one's nothing like Cal. Cal was all about flash and stardust. Danny is the kind of guy who draws people to him without even meaning to. Be mindful.*

'Right, so now that's settled,' Danny said, 'how is old Simone?'

Brooke laughed. Out loud. Her tight breath shooting from her lungs in a delicious wave of relief after being wound up so tight for so long. If Simone had heard him call her old she would have knocked his block off. '*Old* Simone is as painful as ever,' she said.

Danny shifted on the seat, his leg sliding against hers. But in as little time it was gone again. She held her breath until she was sure they were no longer touching. She couldn't tell if he'd even noticed. He merely leaned his elbows back against the bench and looked out through the kitchen windows over his lush garden.

'Why is that? Is it that she's overprotective?' he asked.

'Only to the extent that she can use such behaviour as some kind of weapon.' The moment the words left her mouth Brooke wished she could take them back. 'I'm sorry, I shouldn't have said that.'

'Why not?'

'Because it was mean. And you know her socially so it was unfair.'

He looked her in the eyes when he said, 'For some people it's just their nature to constantly look out for those they love, even if the ones they love don't want it.'

At Danny's turn of phrase Brooke felt a *frisson* shoot up her spine. She wasn't sure what it meant exactly, but she was dead certain it wasn't at all good for her. 'Now it's your turn,' she said, shaking it off.

'To do what exactly?'

'Tell me something you oughtn't. Otherwise I'm going to feel unbalanced all day. And I've had far too many years of yoga to let that happen.'

Danny saw it as the change of subject it was. But he didn't much mind. He was comfortable, she was there, the words were flowing. And when she leant her head on her hand, her hair cascaded in a mass of honey blonde waves down her arm and he knew that even though he had work to do, contacts to go over, phone calls to return, he would sit there talking to her as long as she let him.

'Okay, promise this is as far as this will go,' he said, leaning in closer.

Her eyes widened. 'Wow, I was only kidding. But yes, I promise and cross my heart and all that jazz.'

She shuffled her bottom on the seat and he caught a whiff of her apple-scented shampoo and had to restrain herself from leaning all the way in and burying his nose in her hair.

'Gordon Rose is about to quit football and has been offered a seven figure book deal. And he wants me to act on his behalf.'

Brooke's eyes grew wider with every word. He'd never known a woman who listened like she did. With her whole being. He'd felt it that first day, the first moment they'd had a chance to talk alone. She'd made him feel as if he was the only person in the whole world. Until he'd remembered that she was in fact married to his best friend. But by then it had been too late.

'Wow,' she said. 'I was only hoping for the name of some hulky hetero cricketer who is actually batting for the other team.'

Danny smiled. 'See, all you have to do is give a little and you get a little back.'

'Mmm,' she said. 'Maybe that should become my new philosophy.'

'Your old one being…?'

'Lately? Every man for himself.'

She smiled up at him. He smiled back. And they stayed that way for several really long, really satisfying moments. Sunlight streaming through his huge skylight created myriad colours and textures in her hair. Their knees pointed towards one another. Layers and layers of new revelations wrapping about them. Their relationship shifting and changing until it was already unrecognisable.

He tried to dislodge the sensation that he ought not to have been encouraging cosy, intimate moments like this. They weren't why he'd invited her to stay. He'd done it for Cal, right? In a mixture of looking out for his friend's interests and making up for his friend's mistakes.

Brooke moved first. She sat up straight, cleared her throat and tied her long hair back into a messy knot at the nape of her neck. 'Speaking of the kids, I should check on them.'

'They're okay. Quiet as church mice.'

'Mmm. That's what worries me.' She smiled at him from beneath her lashes and then slid from the stool. He turned on his chair and watched her walk away.

He would have recognised that walk among a million. The slightly boyish figure, the perfect posture, the innocent sway of thin hips and long lean legs. The charming walk of a woman who always thought of herself last. While he thought of her often. Too often.

And thinking the way he was right now was no better than a betrayal of his best friend. The kid who had used his own pocket money to rent Danny his first set of cricket whites in primary school when he'd found out Danny couldn't afford to do so himself. He owed so much to Cal. So much.

He shouldn't be finding ways to touch Brooke. To be near her. To make her smile. To make her like him. It simply couldn't happen. Even if there had always been a connection. An undeniable spark. From the moment their eyes had met across the crowded barbecue he had felt it lodge deep inside him.

A barb that had never let him go. The discomfort he had always felt in her company was sexual tension. Genuine attraction. Pure and simple. Though it wasn't all that pure and far less simple with every passing day.

Even Cal had noticed. He'd only mentioned it once, knowing it need never be mentioned again.

'You're wishing you got there first, aren't you, mate?' Cal had asked after a dinner party one night during those first months.

'If wishes were fishes,' Danny had thrown back.

Cal had grinned, utterly confident in himself and in their friendship. 'Lucky for me they aren't.'

'And never will be,' Danny had promised.

And that was his cross to bear. For even if she walked in here all shining green eyes and lush lips and pink cheeks and skin so soft it physically hurt not to reach out and run his thumb across her cheek, behind her ear and kiss the tip of her straight nose; even if she sat on his lap, dived one hand into the back of his hair, used the other to trace a long silky line down his neck and into the dip of his shirt before leaning in and kissing him senseless... Even then he would not give in.

Cal was gone. But Cal would for evermore be there, between them. And if he hadn't ever been sure that he liked her, he knew he'd always had feelings for her. An involuntary attraction that had never gone away. Feelings that now had to be put back away into the tight, dark, walled-in place inside him where they had been kept for eight long years.

CHAPTER FIVE

LATE that night Brooke walked through the house, switching off lights the kids had left on as they had headed up to bed.

She followed the hum of Danny's deep voice to find him in his study. After the darkness she had left in her wake, his study was like a pool of warmth lit by a banker's lamp on his desk, throwing chunks of shadow and light across a stack of boxes filled with footballs and a tweed couch covered in several framed signed pictures he hadn't found the time to hang.

In contrast, Danny's chiselled profile was lit by the cool glow of his computer screen. He was on the phone. Right leg crossed over left. Swinging back and forth on his big leather chair. Unconsciously rubbing Buckley between his soft ears.

'Funny,' he said suddenly. 'You're a regular comedian.' Though there was no humour in his voice. Enough so that Brooke pulled back and hid in the shadows of the doorway.

'Jeff,' he said. Then, after a pause, again, this time louder, 'Jeff. Stop talking now. Better. Now, listen hard. Jafar's contract is not in the mail. It has not been authorised by your lawyers. It's not even on your to do list for today. How do I know this? I have eyes in the back of my head. I have super-sonic hearing. And I am smarter than you by a factor of ten. So you can't baffle me. Now, if it's not on my desk by ten

Monday morning then Jafar is heading to Sydney on the next plane and the deal's off.'

And then he hung up. Smooth. Slow. One soft click as the slick black phone slid into the cradle. Then, easy as you please, he picked up a piece of paper, flicked it once to hold it stiff, then read over it while rubbing a hand over his chin.

Brooke must have made a noise, must have breathed out the breath she'd been holding, as he suddenly looked up, piercing her with a dark flat stare left over from his recent phone conversation.

But the moment he realised it was her, his gaze softened, warmed, his eyes kind of melting. And if it wasn't for the tension surging through her she might have thought that she had imagined the steely resolve from earlier. But shouldn't that have been the other way around? Danny was all about steely resolve. Warm, soft smiles were the anomaly. Surely.

'What's up?' he asked, leaning forward and resting his forearms on top of his desk. Buckley barked to get more cuddles. 'Scoot,' he said, his voice gentle, and Buckley padded over to a black rug in the corner of the room.

'Just letting you know that I am heading to bed,' Brooke said.

'The kids are asleep?'

'They're beyond asleep. They're practically comatose, thanks to your genius movie marathon and fabulous dinner.' The last of her words were lost inside of a yawn.

'I was about to have a nightcap. Are you too tired to join me?' he asked.

She laughed her way out of her yawn. 'Do I look too tired?'

'Nah,' he said, then he stood and eased around his large desk and joined her at the door. She had to look up to see into his eyes, feeling flat-footed in her bare feet. And small. Tiny really in the shadow of his imposing form.

'The bar's in the den,' he reminded her, when she didn't move, his smile widening, bringing out the tempting dimple. 'I've got to head upstairs for a sec, but I'll join you there in a few minutes.'

'Sure,' she said.

He slid past her. Brooke let out a long wavering gust of air as she watched him jog up the stairs two at a time, all lithe athleticism. She wondered how many times over the next weeks they would find themselves close together in doorways. If anyone was looking on they might think they ended up that way on purpose.

Alone in his study, she decided to take a quick tour. She ended up poring over his bookshelves, because the fun stuff, the truly revealing things, were the knick-knacks a person couldn't bear to throw out. In amongst Danny's treasures, his signed baseballs, his dog-eared back-issues of the *AFL Footy Record,* was only one small framed photograph.

She pulled it out into the muted golden light. It was a photo she'd never seen before; she couldn't even remember it having been taken. But she recognised the scenery as the time Danny and her family had taken a holiday in Barbados when Beau was two.

Those had been the fun years. Just before Cal had become World Champ. Before she had Lily and it became just too hard to travel with him. Before he'd begun to find reasons to stay overseas longer than the race meets required. Before she'd realised she had attached herself to another person who found it too hard to love her.

She ran her finger along Cal's cheek. As per usual he was grinning at the camera, all shining blond hair and big white teeth. A golden boy. In the photo she was turned his way and laughing so hard at something he'd said her hand was clutched to her chest. And Danny…

Brooke's breath hitched in her throat.

He had a look of such delight on his face. Not that same cool practised smile that he usually reserved for photos and television interviews—the one that both hid and promised so much—but a wide smile making best use of his gorgeously crinkled eyes and that sexy solitary dimple. And the thing that seemed to stop her heart was that his smile, all that laughter, all that delight, was projected purely at her.

It could have been the click of the camera accidentally catching him one moment before his eyes skittered past her to Cal who likely had them in stitches with some ribald joke. But perhaps it wasn't…

Brooke slowly put the picture back where she had found it and turned away, and then jumped in fright when she saw Danny leaning against the doorway, the secretive half smile in full evidence.

'Great times, hey?' he said.

'They had their moments.' Brooke knew she must have looked as though she'd been caught with her hand in the cookie jar. She moved away from the mantel and glanced up at the ceiling. 'Is Beau still down?'

'He's asleep in your bed.'

Brooke nodded. 'Lily could sleep atop an active volcano and she wouldn't care, but I thought the first night here might be a bit tough for Beau.'

'Not that *you* want the company, of course,' he said with a smile.

Her gaze tilted downwards and locked with his. Warm, golden brown and glinting with potential for the kind of smile he'd had for her in the photo. Pleasurable tremors thrummed along her skin before settling in her stomach. *Oh, boy*.

'Are you intimating that I am forcing my seven-year-old

to sleep with me as I don't want to sleep alone?' she asked, crossing her arms over the offending area.

'Yep,' he said. 'I know for a fact you used to drag Beau into your bed for the first few nights every time Calvin went away.'

'*He* told you that?' she asked on a shocked whisper.

'This morning, when we were helping the delivery guys, let's say we almost had a "moment" when they tried to take the spare pillow from your bed. Apparently you'd told Beau that could be his pillow whenever he needed it.'

Brooke's heart swelled, and even when it eased back to normal size it still felt beautifully bruised. 'So what did you do?'

Danny thrust his hands into his trouser pockets and the movement threw him into a patch of shadow so that Brooke could no longer see even a hint of light in his dark eyes. 'I packed it into the top of one of your suitcases and forgot to tell you. I took it in to him just now,' he said.

Brooke's overwrought heart tore. She wasn't sure whether she wanted to give Beau a good talking to for not coming to her with his concerns or to run upstairs right now and wrap him up tight and never let him go. And, as for the man standing before her, she had even less of a clue as to how to react to what he had done for her son. 'I think I could do with that nightcap right about now.'

Danny held out a hand and Brooke slid past him, through the huge oval foyer and into the den. She chose a couch and sat down with a thud, the sensation of soft leather against her skin relaxing her no end. It was so comfortable that after the day she'd had she feared she might never want to get back up again.

Danny headed over to the bar and poured two small Scotches into cut-crystal glasses. The clinking sound of ice on glass scurried down her tired nerves. Then instead of taking an armchair, he sat at the other end of the same couch.

'You grew up with just your mum, didn't you?' she asked.

Danny crossed a lazy leg over the other knee. 'I did.'

And he'd turned out pretty okay, she thought. Maybe it was a good thing Beau was here. Not just away from the press, not just safe. But here. With Danny. A guy who knew what he was going through.

'I don't know if I'm more terrified that he's going to start acting out or that he's going to shrink further inside his shell,' she said.

'In my opinion, it's better to be secure in the love of one parent than unsure of two. On that score he's ahead of the game.'

'Mmm,' she said. 'I guess. Though now Lily won't go anywhere without that awful feather boa. It's been three months and counting. I have nightmares of her still wearing it in her university graduation photos.'

Danny laughed, the vibration humming through the couch. Brooke tucked her feet beneath her.

'You're doing fine,' he said. 'Truly. And I promise they'd be a lot worse off if it had gone the other way.'

It took Brooke a few beats to catch on. 'You mean if I had been the one to run my secret sports car over a cliff with some chippie in the passenger seat while gallivanting across Europe as my kids and husband stayed at home?'

Danny took a slow sip of his drink. 'Did it ever occur to you to go that route?'

Brooke blinked. 'The secret sports car or the trip to Europe without the kids? Are you kidding? I fantasized about it every night when I was up feeding Lily and knew I would be doing so on my own for the next month at least.'

Danny smiled but it didn't reach his eyes, for he had noticed that she had quite purposely misunderstood him. 'I imagine if it had been me I would have wanted to give Cal a taste of his own medicine. You never considered straying?'

'Straying. Put like that, you make it sound kind of accidental.' And easy, she thought. Especially in the quiet semi-darkness of the low-lit room.

She slumped lower in the chair and took a long leisurely sip of the aged Scotch, relishing the burning sensation lighting her lungs and loosening her tongue. 'I don't know where I would have met anyone worth straying with. My social life for so many years has consisted of mothers' groups, parent-teacher meetings and the doctor's office. So I guess that idea was a non-starter.'

'Is that your reason? Or is it the same reason you are still wearing your wedding ring?' he asked, though his eyes never once left hers.

Brooke realised she had been playing with it for some time, twirling it around her ring finger using the thumb of the same hand. It wasn't something she normally did. She barely noticed it any more. She'd worn the thing for eight years. Almost a third of her life.

'Have you thought about when you might take it off?' he asked, watching her as he took another sip of his drink.

'You're all about the hard questions tonight, aren't you?' She let her hand drop away, though she could still feel the warmth beneath the gold.

He merely smiled. 'You miss him still, don't you?'

She breathed in and out through her nose. 'At times, like crazy,' she admitted. 'It's odd. It had been some time since our relationship was rosy, and he was never home anyway. But it's like I could always reach out my thoughts and find him wherever he was. I could picture him somewhere keeping a room full of people entertained. It was somehow comforting. Now I reach out and...there's nothing.'

She sniffed and blinked to clear the fuzz that had smeared her vision. Then she laughed, nervously pulling her hair into a tight high ponytail and then letting it fall over the back of the couch. 'Does that make me sound ridiculous?'

'Nah,' Danny drawled. 'I know exactly what you mean. Even now, when the phone rings late at night, my first thought is that it's him, somewhere overseas, with no idea what the time is back here. He was the last guy you'd count on for a lift home at the end of a big night but you couldn't help but love him anyway.'

Brooke slid her feet to the floor and cradled her drink between both hands. 'And here I am feeling all sorry for myself. How are you holding up?'

'I'm…coming to terms with it.' He smiled, and this time it was lit with self-deprecation, making him seem more human somehow. And closer all the while. Had he moved? Or had she? Either way, she was close enough to see a ring of dark chocolate-brown around his golden irises.

'If you ever want to talk about him…' she offered.

'Then I won't hesitate,' he said.

Her drink wasn't finished but it had done its job. She felt warm, calm, ready for a good night's sleep. She stood and Danny's chin rose as he watched her. 'I think it's time I get to bed, or I might just sleep where I fall. Are you heading up now?'

Danny shook his head. 'Not yet. I have a bit of work to catch up on.'

Brooke grimaced. 'Our fault?'

'Not at all. I'm glad I was able to do this for you. And I'm glad you're here.'

'Me too,' she decided.

Danny laid his glass next to hers on the heavy wood coffee table and stood as well. He put his hands into the dip at his lower back and stretched, pushing his broad chest forward, the muscles of his upper arms straining against his shirt sleeves. She found herself staring, and took that as her cue to leave.

She walked to the doorway, but turned back at the last second. Holding on to the frame for support, she said, 'I know you've never really warmed to me.'

She waited for him to protest, to give some clue that Simone was right, or that the smile in the photo had truly been for her, but he didn't even flinch. Incongruously, that made her feel more at ease than she had all day.

'As such, I appreciate what you have done for us today all the more. You're a good man, Danny Finch.'

He nodded. Just once.

And then she turned and walked away.

The next morning Brooke padded downstairs in her Winnie-the-Pooh pyjamas, her hair pulled up into its usual night-time concoction of two high ponytails that by morning made her look like a bedraggled poodle.

She hadn't slept so well in weeks. The bed in the room Danny had given her was like something out of a dream. It was huge and soft with pillows made of down feathers and sheets that slid over her body like silk. Beau and Lily were both in there now, asleep together.

She rubbed both fists into her eyes as she trudged into the kitchen to find Danny sitting at the round kitchen table already dressed in his usual black suit and leaning back reading a newspaper lit by great swathes of glorious morning sunshine pouring through the ceiling-to-floor windows.

Brooke slumped into a chair next to his, hooking one foot up on to the seat so that she could hug her knee for balance. She reached over and stole half a piece of toast lathered in avocado, mayonnaise and lemon juice.

Danny closed the newspaper and glanced at her. He gave her a quick once-over and his mouth kicked into a half smile and his right eyebrow hooked upwards.

'Why are you looking at me like that?' Brooke asked with a mouthful of food.

'Like what?'

'Like I have avocado on my face.'

Danny folded the newspaper, then let it fall to the table. 'Maybe because that avocado was at one stage my avocado and I'm trying to decide what lengths I might go to in order to get it back.'

Brooke swallowed. 'You're loaded. You can afford to get another avocado.' She took another bite of toast and breathed through her nose while she dragged herself further awake.

'But what if I only want *that* avocado?'

Brooke stopped chewing. She had the funny feeling they were suddenly talking about two different things, but she was still too sleepy to be sure. 'There are plenty more avocados…in the sea. Get over it and move on with your life.'

He reached out and tugged on one of her poodle ears. 'Are you always this chirpy in the morning?'

'I should warn you,' she said while pulling her messy ponytail back into place, 'it takes me a good half hour and a strong cup of coffee to become the calm, cool, collected mother of the year you know and love. Until that time I am noxious.'

His smile twitched and Brooke thought maybe she ought to have kept her mouth shut before that half hour was over. But she wasn't all that used to having to make conversation with anyone other than a grumbly Beau and a manic Lily in the mornings.

Danny pulled himself out of his chair and took his folded newspaper with him into the kitchen proper.

Brooke leant her face against her palm. If she looked bedraggled first thing in the morning, he looked the complete opposite. He looked smooth, crisp, ready to take on the world. She wasn't sure if she felt envious of his efficiency or whether the tumbling in her stomach was a purely female reaction to the sight of a guy in his prime. Of course it could have just been indigestion from eating the toast too fast.

He rinsed a couple of dishes and put them in the shiny black dishwasher straight away. Pure female appreciation surged through her that had nothing to do with indigestion. She laughed at herself. If a guy doing his own chores could turn her on, that truly showed how half-asleep she still was.

She popped the last bite into her mouth and chewed more slowly. And admitted to herself that if not for the stubbornness and coolness and general disinclination to talk about himself, ever, and the standing with the fridge door open for long periods thing, he really would be some catch. For some lucky girl. Some day…

Unless, of course, he already had some lucky girl. That was a possibility. She hadn't known he lived in a fairy tale house in a forest—what else didn't she know?

'Do you have any other regular guests we ought to know about?' she asked. 'Or who ought to know about us?'

He glanced up at her, his eyes narrowed in confusion.

'Like, maybe, perhaps a regular female-type guest.'

His eyes went back to their normal shape and his mouth slid into the kind of smile that made her need to take a deeper breath. 'Are you asking if I am currently seeing anybody?'

'I guess I am,' she said.

He glanced quickly to flick the kettle on to boil. 'I did have a very nice dinner date two nights ago.'

Brooke coughed on her toast. 'But you were at our place at the crack of dawn yesterday.' Meaning he couldn't have spent the night with...whoever she was. Not the whole night anyway. By the twinkle in his eye he knew exactly what she was thinking.

'Does she have a name?' Brooke asked, figuring *in for a penny...*

Danny grabbed a black ceramic bowl and filled it with cornflakes and milk. 'She does. And it's Emily.'

Brooke uncurled herself from the chair and moved to take a seat at the barstool on the other side of the bench. 'First date?'

He pushed the cereal her way, then followed through with a spoon. 'Actually, no.'

Huh. Well, what do you know? When she'd started in on this conversation it truly had never occurred to her that he was seeing someone. Not that she'd imagined him at home sitting by the phone awaiting her next desperate phone call. Well, okay, so she kind of had. He'd always been there for her when she'd needed him before. But still, she hadn't imagined there was an *Emily* in his life.

A flash of silver cut across her vision and Brooke realised he was still holding her spoon. Actually he was waving it back and forth like a hypnotist. She reached out and grabbed it.

'And where did you two lovebirds meet?' Even she heard the sarcasm in her voice. She dug her spoon deep into her cereal rather than look straight into those far-too-alert brown eyes.

'The mid-season fundraising ball for a local football team,' he said. 'She's on the board.'

He grabbed the pot of coffee and poured her a mug before adding the perfect amount of milk and half a teaspoon of sugar. It occurred to her that it had been years since she'd had to tell him how she liked her coffee. At some stage he'd begun to simply know.

She chewed and swallowed and left her spoon resting in the bowl. 'So you two are an item, then,' she said. 'For real.'

Danny pushed the mug over to her, then leant his palms on the bench. 'I guess that depends on what constitutes a couple being an item these days.'

'You're asking me?' she said, flattening a hand against her chest. 'A woman who hasn't been on a date in…eight-odd years?'

He nodded. 'I am. Some day soon you will be out there again and you are going to have to know these things.'

'Out where?' she asked, her hand jerking.

'On the market. Dating. New men.' His last words came to her low and slow. Bringing about mental images of manly things like muscles, and clever hands, and the musky scent of a bathroom after a guy showered. It was unnerving to say the least. Especially unnerving because her reaction to such thoughts wasn't so much the expected dread, as it was cut through with a surge of anticipation.

She shook her head. 'Oh, no. Not me. I'm done with all that jazz.'

She thought Danny was not going to comment. He didn't say anything for such a very long time. But finally he asked, 'And why's that?'

'Apart from being so rusty that I squeak, I've been a mother for so long I don't think I would even know how to be somebody's girlfriend again. I mean first dates, getting to know you blather, finding a way to tell a guy that no matter how much he enjoys nuzzling against your ear you in fact can't stand it.' A shiver racked her body.

Danny laughed. A deep resounding rumble that washed over her skin until her toes tingled. He uncoiled from his imposing leaning-on-the-bench pose to put the milk back in the fridge. It gave her a good long moment to shake out her hands and get some much needed oxygen into her lungs.

'It's not all that bad,' he said. 'Finding someone you are attracted to, who can keep up one half of an intelligent conversation, who likes the things you like, is one of the great pleasures in life.'

The way he said the word *pleasures* created goose bumps along Brooke's arms. It was as though her body was out of her control. Another fifteen minutes and a good dose of coffee and she'd be back in charge. 'So is that why you have never settled down yourself? You like the thrill of new great pleasures too much?'

His half-cocked smile shifted into the full-blown version and Brooke wished she hadn't asked. All those warm tumbling feelings normally associated with brimming attraction, with nice first dates and expectant trips up the front steps after such evenings came swimming back to her in such a flood of awareness she couldn't even hope to stop them. She wrapped her hands around her coffee and stared blindly into its brown depths.

'Like many single men,' he said, 'I have not yet settled as I have never found a woman with whom I can imagine remaining for the rest of my life. The day that happens she will be the last woman I will ever kiss. The last I will ever wrap my arms around and the last one in whose length I will bury myself as I drift off to sleep. I don't see how anyone can make that decision lightly.'

Brooke dragged her eyes upwards to find he had taken a cloth and was slowly running it up and down the length of the bench, wiping away invisible crumbs. She swallowed to wet her suddenly dry throat.

Danny was meant to be big, brash and stubborn. He was meant to be her safety net. Her cushion against landing butt first on the cold hard ground. He was not meant to be a closet romantic, a poet, a wannabe lover. Adding those layers to all she already knew about him made him suddenly seem...dangerous.

'Do you believe that?' Brooke asked. She had to discreetly clear a frog from her throat before adding, 'That people can be heart, body and soul, until the end of time faithful?'

His hand stilled. He blinked once. Twice. He rinsed the cloth, squeezed out the excess water and folded it neatly over his long silver tap. Then he turned and looked her in the eye, all previous smiles gone as he considered her words with such serious deliberation she found herself hanging on his answer with such need she couldn't breathe.

'I do,' he finally said. 'Despite much evidence to the contrary, I believe in happily ever afters. I believe that the right two people can be happily monogamous until they are old and grey. The problem is so many couples nowadays settle for the wrong reasons rather than waiting to find that one right person. And that can only end badly.'

Blunt as you please, he was talking about her. And Cal. And sure, a million other couples out there in the world who were struggling to keep it together. But right then and there he was mostly talking about her.

Had she settled? Had she grabbed on to the first half-baked chance she'd found? Had her desperation to be in a relationship, a partnership, not alone but not under her sister's wing, sent her leaping into Cal's open arms? When if she'd waited... she would not have Beau and Lily in her life. They flat-out negated every other regret she could ever hope to have.

She reached across the bench and grabbed the newspaper, fiddling with its corner, using it as a distraction.

'So *are* you and Emily an item?' she asked again. But this

time she knew she was really asking if this woman was the last woman Danny would ever kiss, wrap his arms around at night and love.

He watched her some more, his golden gaze flickering over every inch of her face before it landed back on her eyes. She couldn't have looked away if her life depended on it. Her joints felt weak. Her face hot. Her toes bloodless. What was she doing? What was *he* doing?

'Emily and I are very close,' he said.

And Brooke realised *he* was doing nothing at all. Every last skerrick of breath slid from her lungs in one long silent sigh. It seemed that while she had been caught up in her own mini-tragedy of a life, some lucky girl had already found him. Which was a good thing. A great thing. He deserved it. And more.

She cricked her neck to the left. 'Well, good for you. And for Emily. My advice would be to hang on tight. The course of true love is far more fragile than you could even imagine.'

She shot him a chummy smile before drinking down half her coffee in one hit. It seared the back of her throat and burnt off a good layer of tastebuds, but she didn't much care. At least it brought familiar feeling back to her consciousness rather than all the weird tumbly befuddlement she had been experiencing.

Black ink smudges on her white mug brought her attention back to the fresh newspaper. She gazed at the headlines and pictures, not really seeing them, until...

She slid off the kitchen stool, her hands flying off the paper as though it had burned.

Danny swore beneath his breath and she knew then that he'd already seen the article hidden in the bottom corner of the back page of the newspaper.

She ran both hands over her eyes, bringing herself fully awake. But it was all still there when she looked back.

FINDLAY WIDOW MOVES ON

The *double entendre* was obvious, especially considering the accompanying photo. It had been taken as they had made the mad dash from her house to Danny's car the day before. To the innocent observer it made them look like a family. She with Lily in her arms, Danny with Beau in his.

She glanced up at Danny, whose stance showed he was prepared for anything. Flying crockery, tears, another fainting spell. Well, she wasn't going to give him the satisfaction.

'Brooke, it's nothing,' he said. 'It's a filler. It's buried in sports. In the level of importance in a newspaper, this would be considered a non-story. So what does it matter?'

'What does it matter?' she threw back at him. 'As far as they are concerned, I should be grieving for the man I loved and instead they think I have shacked up with his best mate.'

'Brooke, it doesn't matter—'

'It matters,' she finished. 'Don't you get it? I hadn't *seen* Cal in over six months. The last time we talked was when he rang from Italy to say he wouldn't be home for Beau's birthday. Hell, we hadn't even slept together in over a year. Maybe I should just call this journalist and tell him that.'

The room fell silent, her words echoing off the far walls. She felt rather than saw Danny flinch. And she didn't blame him. It wasn't as if she had meant to share that last snippet. But she needed somebody to know her side. To know she wasn't living out a soap opera. She was hurt. And lost. And real.

She ran a hand over her forehead. 'I'm sorry. That's probably more information than you were counting on.'

'You have nothing to be sorry for, Brooke.'

She jabbed a finger at the offending article. 'But they don't know that. God, I wish—'

'If wishes were fishes,' Danny said, his voice so cool, so

calm, it ran over her skin like a balm, slicing the edges off her anger. 'I'm sure we all would have done a lot of things differently over the years.'

We. He'd said *we*. As though he had regrets. And the way he was looking at her right now, she just knew that they involved her.

Suddenly Brooke didn't want to play any more. In case she made him regret being there for her. Or worse, in case he regretted not being there for her more.

She leaned over the bench and tipped the remainder of her coffee into the sink. 'That's it, Danny. We're out of here.'

'Don't be ridiculous.'

'I don't need this. You don't need this. You're the PR genius. Imagine how your business will suffer if every client thinks that you are just biding your time before you make a move on their wife or girlfriend.'

She tried to leave, but he reached out and grabbed her by the arm, his fingers pinching into her bicep. She jolted to a stop. But the pressure instantly eased until she could have slipped away if she had wanted to.

She tilted her chin and glared up into his eyes. Golden. Intense. Lion's eyes, which made her rethink her position, which made her want to just give in and lean on him for evermore.

'Don't go,' he said.

'I should,' she whispered.

'Should isn't a reason. Should is pandering to some imagining of what others think you ought to do. Stay because you want to. Stay because you need to. Stay because this is the best place for you right now.'

'Then invite Emily over,' she shot back.

Danny's brow furrowed.

'I mean it,' she said, fighting against heavier-than-normal

breaths. 'I'm not kidding, Danny. Invite her over here and quick. For dinner. Please.'

'Fine,' he finally said, and let her go.

She took a step back from him. Two. But she could still feel the tension pulsing off him in waves, bathing her in his heat. She knew she ought to take her leave. Leave him with her half-eaten cornflakes and dirty coffee mug and go check on the kids. Have a cold shower. Hide under the duvet for another fifteen minutes.

But she simply found she couldn't. Not while he was standing there watching her, his eyes brimming with concern, the same way he had looked at her when she had awoken from her faint. He looked at her as if he cared. Deeply.

And it had just been so long since she'd been on the receiving end of such a look. Too damn long.

Danny couldn't move either. He was petrified to the spot.

Brooke's hair was a shaggy mess, her pyjamas crumpled, her wide green eyes framed by sexy smudges of dark eyeliner she hadn't washed away properly the night before. She hadn't needed to prance around the kitchen in her underwear to leave him breathless; she just needed to show up.

He should have just let her go. He could have put her up in a hotel for as long as she needed. Hell, he could have sent her to the Bahamas for a month to keep her out of the public eye if that truly was his intent.

But he wanted her near. He'd wanted her near for as long as he could remember. And, now he had her, he wondered how much harder it would be to let her go. For he would have to let her go. For a hundred different reasons.

He was putting more on the line than she even realised. If her staying with him really did become a story, the corporate respect he had spent years building could be put into jeopardy.

She had never shown him any real signs of interest to begin with, so begging her to stay would achieve nothing more than prolonging his own torture. Added to that, she was his best friend's wife. Always would be.

And she was a single mum and there was no way he would mess with that kind of relationship unless he was planning on sticking around for the long haul. He'd been there each time his mum had settled on a new guy. And every time it had fallen apart he'd had to pick up the pieces.

The only reason swaying the balance, the only reason for him not to let her go, to convince her to stay, was that he could no longer deny that he adored her. He prized her moods, her spirit, her ferocious desire to care for her kids above all else. It hurt him to see her struggle and he felt her victories as though they were his own. He was so attracted to her it physically hurt. But was that reason enough to fight? Or all the more reason to send her away?

Now was not the time to push for those answers. Now was the time to calm her down and make her feel safe. That was his promise to her, one he intended to keep.

'Now that's settled, what are your plans for today?' he asked, amazed that his voice didn't sound as tight as his throat felt.

'I hadn't thought past yesterday, to tell you the truth,' she said, her voice cool, her eyes wary. Her shoulders were so tight it took all of his strength not to take the two long strides to her side to run his hands over her shoulders, ease out the knots, make her body go limp under his ministrations.

'I have to go into Melbourne for a few hours this morning. Will you be okay here on your own?'

'Of course,' she said, squaring her shoulders some more, trying to look like the epitome of control, which in her messy pigtails and Winnie-the-Pooh pyjamas she had no hope of pulling off.

'I'll leave you the keys to my little runabout Audi in case you and the kids want to go out. They'd love Miss Marple's in Sassafras. Or you could take them on the Puffing Billy steam train. But, if not, the fridge is fully stocked. Or I can leave you some cash for takeout…'

'No,' she said.

'No to which part exactly?'

'No cash.'

'Twenty bucks isn't going to break me, Brooke.'

'I made some money selling our furniture. Enough to keep us in food and clothes for a while. And I told you before, I won't accept charity from anybody.' She blinked, her huge green eyes glassy, and…scared? Of what? Never finding her feet again?

Danny felt the air fade from his lungs. How had this woman ended up with so little faith? In herself or in others. It couldn't have just been from Cal, could it?

He leant forward, not saying anything until she glanced up at him from beneath her too pretty for her own good eyelashes. 'I'm not just anybody, Brooke.'

She swallowed. And stared right on back. Finally her shoulders slumped. She even found it in herself to dredge up a smile. 'I know you're not. But you've done more than enough to help. I don't know quite what I've ever done to deserve it.'

She took a step forward and reached out and laid a hand over his. Her cool fingers wrapping gently around his.

'But no cash, not ever. I can't think myself that broken,' she said, sliding her hand away and leaving his own hand feeling naked.

She breathed in deep through her nose and out through her mouth, then shook out her arms like a swimmer about to dive into a cold lake. 'Speaking of the kids, I'd better go give them a hurry up.'

Danny nodded. 'I'll be off, then. I'll see you some time this afternoon.'

She smiled and walked away. Not intimating that she would be looking forward to his return, or was glad to see him go.

He clenched his fist so hard he bruised his palm. God! Why her? Why couldn't he have fallen for some sweet young thing who adored him right on back years ago?

He'd dated celebrated blondes, brainy brunettes, ravishing redheads. And then there was Emily, his good friend and sometimes dinner companion. She was a fabulous woman. Smart, funny, beautiful, working in the same field as he was. And a good sport who had realised that the two of them would never be more than friends before he had.

So why hadn't he been able to make a real go of it with any of them?

Why? He knew why.

Because not one of them was Brooke Findlay.

CHAPTER SIX

IT HAD been one hell of a day.

With the football season drawing to a close, Danny's workload was growing. The player draft was just around the corner, several of his top-notch current list were out of contract, feigning moves to rival clubs or seriously thinking about it, and it was all up to him to look out for their interests using any means necessary. Smoke and mirrors. Distraction and rumour. Veiled threats and whispered promises.

It was a blood sport and he loved it. And for five years now he had been by far the best there was. He played to win. Always. And in most areas of his life he had succeeded. Bar one.

It was the same reason that had him leaving work early. That afternoon, as glorious sunshine outside his office window hit the waters of Port Philip Bay just so, something else called to him more. Somewhere else. Someone else.

Once home, Danny threw his keys on to the kitchen bench and grabbed an apple from the fruit bowl before realising it was the first time it had held fruit in…well, ever. Rather than collecting dust and junk mail on his counter, it now held a huge mound of apples, oranges and big, firm, ripe avocados.

'Brooke,' he said out loud, a smile tickling at his cheeks. He stretched his ears to hear if she was still home. He heard wind slapping against his kitchen windows and the customary creaks and groans of a house that wasn't brand-new. And finally he heard a squeal.

Lily. He turned to see a blonde head of curls framed by a pink feather boa streaming past his kitchen window. He sauntered around the bench in time to see Beau tearing behind her. And after him came Buckley, tongue lolling, frolicking like a puppy.

And, last of all, came Brooke. Short khaki shorts showing off long, lean, tanned legs; bare feet with newly bright-pink toenails; long hair in low pigtails to match her daughter's; and a *Little Mermaid* tank top wrapped tight to her slim torso showcasing curves enough to turn any man's head.

'We're coming to get you,' Danny heard Beau say with all the eerie depth of a character in a horror film, showing not a hint of the scared little boy from the day before.

Lily panicked and crouched in the middle of the lush lawn and covered her head with her boa and squealed, half in fear and half in delight that she was about to be caught.

Brooke rushed at her daughter and grabbed her. Then Beau tackled them both until they rolled on the lush grass, tickling and giggling as Brooke covered them with kisses until they were both squealing. Overwhelmed by all the excitement, Buckley ran away to chase something invisible into the immense forest at the side of the house.

Danny breathed in deep through his nose. This was the reason he had come home early. This was the one facet his life had been missing. This glorious earth mother with a beauty so natural she could have graced the pages of any high fashion magazine, but instead had chosen a family life. She'd chosen it and stuck by it, putting her own life on hold to stay with a philandering husband so that her kids could grow up happy.

When the rumours had started about Cal's extra-curricular

activities, many in the press had vilified her for taking it on the chin. But Danny had thought otherwise. He'd been astounded by her humility. Her self-sacrifice. And tremendous inner strength. It took some kind of grace to ride that kind of wave of negativity and come out the other end heroic.

Drawn to the scene outside like a nine iron to a new golf ball, Danny pulled his tie undone and draped it over the back of a kitchen chair, shuffled his jacket off his shoulders, placing it over the same chair, undid his top two buttons and headed outside.

At the sound of the sliding door opening, all squealing and smooching stopped and three similar faces looked his way.

'Danny,' Lily called out. 'Help me! They're trying to kill me to death.'

'No, we're not,' Beau said, scoffing at his little sister. 'You're so melodramatic.'

Brooke disentangled herself from her kids' limbs, stood and brushed herself down, running swift hands over her tight tank top, her shorts, her long smooth legs. A few grass clippings remained on the outside of her left thigh. Danny thought about walking over to her, reaching down and flicking them away. Then he thought about it some more.

'Race you to the swing, Lil,' Beau said, and was already halfway to the old black tyre on a rope that hung from the horizontal branch of an elm tree before Lily managed to get to her feet.

Brooke let them be, and wandered over to him. Her hair was a shambles. Her tank top had slid slightly off one shoulder, revealing the strap of a lacy pink bra. The green depths of her eyes were as dark and mysterious as the rainforest backdrop. She was utterly and completely gorgeous.

She glanced briefly at his open collar before her gaze

skidded back up to his eyes. 'Hi,' she said, her voice ragged from her recent exertion.

'Hi,' he said back, undoing his cuff buttons and rolling his shirt sleeves up to the elbows. 'I didn't mean to interrupt.'

She waved a hand in front of her face and leant her hands on her thighs while she regained her breath. 'I'm glad you did. I'm exhausted. This is about the eighth time today we've played chasey.'

'Sounds like a good day to me.'

'Considering everything, it really has been.' And then she smiled, truly smiled, creating shadows beneath her high cheekbones and gathering flecks of sunshine in her eyes. Danny knew he could put up with a lot to be on the receiving end of such smiles.

'Simone called me at work today,' he said, before he did or said something stupid. But when her smile faded, her eyes clouded, he realised it was too late for that.

'Why?' she said, standing and shielding her eyes from the sun with an open palm.

'To check up on you, I expect.' *And me,* he thought, though he thought better about saying that there had been a definite threat of injury and possibly even castration if he let anything bad happen to Brooke while under his care. 'So I invited her and Jerry around for dinner tonight.'

'You what?' Brooke asked, her voice sharp. Too sharp. He knew that she and Simone had their differences, but she looked downright terrified at the thought of her sister coming to dinner.

'Is there a problem?'

'I just…I wish you'd asked me first.'

'Sorry. Next time I will.'

'Next time?' she repeated, and the clouds in her eyes thankfully disappeared as she let her hand drop. She smiled slightly, letting the sun in, letting him in.

Yeah, next time. Like dinner parties could happen again and often. Forever… 'Sure,' he said. 'They can come any time you like. Anyone you like can come any time you like.'

'Once will be more than enough,' she said, 'I can assure you. The only reason you continue to take her calls is that you have only had her in small doses. I, on the other hand, have no choice.'

Lily squealed and they both looked up to find her hanging on to the tyre while Beau gently rocked it back and forth.

'The swing is a success,' he said.

'Big time. Though if you tell me that you built it yourself before buying *The Lion King* DVD then I think I'm going to hit you.'

Danny smiled back. She made it an easy feat. 'No fear. It was here when I bought the place. I've thought about taking it down. Just never got around to it.'

'I'm glad you didn't. The kids have been on there half the morning. You never thought you'd have kids here one day to use it?'

She placed her hands in the small of her back as she stretched tall, thrusting her breasts forward in such a manner that Danny watched her kids playing so as not to be caught staring.

'I think it's a big decision to bring a child into the world. You have to be really sure of your own position in it first,' he said.

She nodded. Her eyes full of understanding. And he wondered how much Cal had told her about his own less than exemplary childhood. Plenty, he realised as her smile softened and drew him in.

'I'm with you there,' she said. 'But, then again, how cool would it be to have a backyard cricket team at your disposal any time you wanted it?'

Danny laughed, layer upon layer of stress just melting away. 'There is that. Though the current affairs TV shows like to tell us kids these days prefer video games to outdoor pursuits.'

'What will become of people like you in the future if kids stop playing sports?'

'Ah, now you see there'll always be some kids who play sports. It will just be harder to find the good ones. They will be worth more. They will need more guidance to field the offers they will get. Therefore, I will hold all the cards.'

She laughed, the husky sound fading too fast in the wide open space. 'There really is no bounds to your confidence, is there?'

He braved a glance forward to find she had crossed her arms across her chest. Much better for his equilibrium. 'Is there something wrong with that?'

'Well, there can be. Cal for one was always overconfident. I believe it was his greatest attraction and greatest flaw.'

'Are you warning me to take heed?'

Her smile grew but it didn't light her eyes. 'I don't know that I am. I don't think it defines you the same way it did him.'

'And that's a good thing?'

'Oh, yeah,' she said with such vehemence Danny found the need to stretch his neck and shift his feet and generally do his all not to ask her to repeat her words with exactly that intonation a dozen more times.

'Perhaps I ought to hire you to do my PR,' he said.

She laughed again but kept her attention on her kids. 'It would be money for nothing,' she said. 'You don't need PR. You're smart, successful and far too good-looking for your own good. And having us to stay only shows that you are truly a saint. I'm not sure what kind of spin could offer any improvement.'

He warmed at her playfulness. It reminded him how they had been in the beginning, years before—niggling, baiting, pushing each other's boundaries until Cal had to separate them before a full-in brawl ensued.

'Sounds to me like you've thought about it,' he said, wondering where the boundaries might be now that Cal wasn't around to referee.

'Mmm,' she said. 'Though there is one small thing that makes me wonder if I haven't missed some great flaw.'

'And that is?'

'Why any woman hasn't managed to snap you up as yet. I know you have your Emily on the string at the moment, but as far as I can tell there has been no exchange of rings? Or promises?'

He shook his head. And though this conversation could fast turn dangerous if she managed to follow her thoughts through to their correct conclusion—that the reason was right in front of him—at the moment she was playing. And he simply couldn't resist that smile. 'And what did you decide?'

She turned slightly to face him and her smile grew. 'I have a few theories.'

'Which are?'

'Well,' she drawled, flicking a glance towards the kids, who were happily swinging the tyre around the tree trunk and then running away as it uncurled itself. 'Taking into account all I know about you—'

'My smarts, my success and my... What was the other part?' He lifted one innocent eyebrow.

Her cheeks went pink. Her mouth hooked into an indifferent half smile. But at least she looked him in the eye as she said, 'Your unsurpassed good looks.'

'Right. Of course.' He waved a magnanimous hand in the air. 'Do go on.'

'Considering all of that, the only reason you have not

been snapped up *must* be due to a lack of skill in the bedroom department.'

Her words came thick and fast, and once she was finished the world turned quiet. The birds seemed to still. The wind stopped rustling through the trees. The only thing Danny could hear was the quickening beat of his own heart.

'You have been thinking, long and hard, about my prowess in the bedroom,' he repeated, so enjoying the flush spreading across Brooke's soft cheeks, the clenching of her jaw, the fight in her eyes as she mentally chastised herself for giving in to what amounted to an instinctive desire to torment him. He bit back the urge to laugh.

'Hey, don't turn this on me,' she said. 'You're the one with the lack of skill.'

Danny didn't even begin to rise to the bait. He was utterly confident of his skill in that area of his life. It matched—hell, it even surpassed—his much-lauded skills in other areas of his life. He'd dated, and dated, and dated, as much for the enjoyment as for the effort of putting this very woman as far out of his head as possible. And he'd learnt a thing or two about how to please. Nothing this cheeky minx said would make him think otherwise. 'So, during these long, hard thoughts of yours, what have you decided I ought to do about this supposed flaw in my general perfection?'

'I hear there are tapes,' she said, her shoulders relaxing as she once more got into the swing of things. 'And courses. I'm sure we could find something for you at a local adult learning centre.'

Finally he gave in to the urge to laugh. It rolled through him, loosening his chest, warming his limbs, making his cheeks feel stretched out.

'So how close to the mark am I?' she asked, the amusement in her voice making it soft, intimate and sexy as hell.

He looked down at her, revelling in the eye contact, in how it sliced through him, right through him, like no one else had ever been able to do. He wondered how easy it would be to please this woman. But he didn't have to wonder long. He knew pleasing her would be the most natural thing in the whole world.

'Brooke, honey,' he said, 'you are so far off the mark it would blow your mind.'

She blinked as his words sank in. Her throat worked as she swallowed, but she never once looked away. 'Well then, it's probably lucky for me, and my future dating prospects *out there,* that I'll never really know for sure.'

Then she released him from her levelling gaze and jogged over to the relative safety of her kids. 'Who wants a push?' she asked.

'Me!' they called out in unison.

Danny took in a deep breath, filling his lungs. He felt as though he had just discovered nooks and crannies inside them which he'd never known were there. Nooks and crannies filled by her. By this tension and hunger that pervaded him every time he was around her. Hell, every time he had been around her since the moment they had met.

He undid another button and tugged his shirt from his trousers, loosening his clothes until he felt as if he could breathe again, and then slowly edged over towards the tree.

Watching Beau and Lily laugh and play, he couldn't remember any days like this from his own childhood. He had grown up in apartments. With no space. No yard. No trees. Small patches of concrete out the back near the industrial bins were the only places where kids could play. And the landlords affixed signs to filthy brick walls saying: 'No graffiti. No skateboards. No loitering.' They may as well have written 'No hope' for all the encouragement it gave.

In comparison these kids would be fine. When Brooke found a home for them, even without all the space and comfort and video projector and Buckley, they would be fine. He had no doubt. Because they had her. But how would he be? When Brooke finally left and took her kids with her, would he evermore hear the echo of their laughter, reminding him of the domestic life he had deliberately never made for himself?

He shook it off. For with Brooke barefoot and frolicking in his backyard, with her kids laughing, forgetting that anything bad existed outside this moment, today, right now, there was sunshine and vitality. Laughter and merriment. Simplicity and time spread out before him.

'Do you guys want to play a game of tennis?' he called out, the need to be involved bursting through his conscientious reserve.

'Sure!' Beau said, since he wasn't the one in the tyre at that moment.

'Sure!' Lily repeated, pulling herself from the tyre's grip.

'How about you, Brooke?' he asked. 'We can't play doubles with only three of us. Needs to be four of us to make it count. Are you with me?'

And when she looked up at him, her eyes eclipsed by the shadow of the large elm, and said, 'Sure,' it took every ounce of Danny's sense not to read more into that one small word than he wanted to.

Especially since he had noticed the moment he'd joined her on the grass that she was no longer wearing her wedding ring.

Danny was as serious a sportsman as he was a businessman.

But as he stood on his tennis court ten minutes later in his purpose-bought, black Nike T-shirt and shorts, he had the horrible feeling the match would not go according to plan.

Brooke was still barefoot. Lily now wore a tutu over her clothes as that was apparently what all girl tennis players wore. And Beau was bouncing the strings of the racket against his head. Over and over again. It was actually mesmerising. Boing, boing, boing. How the kid wasn't getting a headache, Danny had no idea.

'Do you guys even know how to play tennis?' he called out, dreading the answer.

Brooke glanced up from where she was twisting Lily's tutu around to face the right way. 'Beau's had some lessons at school this year. And Lily and I have watched lots on TV, haven't we, Lil?'

'Yessssss,' Lily said, watching her tutu spin as she twirled around with glee.

'Right,' Danny muttered. 'This is going to be interesting.'

'Boys versus girls,' Beau called out, running to stand on Danny's side of the net.

Danny's right eye began to twitch. Those with some skill versus those with none. He wished hard for a sudden thunderstorm so that they couldn't partake in his bright idea. But the beautiful blue September sky didn't look promising.

Danny was about to explain the finer points of the game when Lily rushed to the net, grabbed on with both hands and tried to poke her tongue through the holes, and he gave up. It was either that or suffer a stress aneurism on the spot.

'Beau can serve first,' Danny said, rolling a couple of fast balls the kid's way.

Beau missed one, his face screwing up with frustration until he caught the second. Catastrophe averted. He shuffled his right leg forward and placed the ball atop his racket, then glared sternly at his mum across the net.

Brooke had the racket clasped in both hands. She was bent

from the waist, feet a good shoulder-width apart, and she rocked her pert backside back and forth, concentration etched on her face.

He didn't know whether to laugh or be turned on. In the end he simply gave in to both.

Beau threw the ball in the air and hit it. The kid had fantastic motion, Danny thought. Not much strength, for he was a scrawny mite, but his action was spot on. Natural. His earlier reticence had disappeared; maybe some good could come of this after all.

His gaze swung to Brooke. She bounced up on to her toes, her thick blonde pigtails swinging, all gloss and warmth and beauty. And as the ball bounced directly her way she closed her eyes and swung with such force that she spun on the spot.

And missed. By a good foot below the trajectory of the ball.

Danny let out a shot of hot breath. This was going to be a long afternoon.

Brooke came out of her spin, her eyes bright. 'I missed!' she said, with as much pleasure as if she'd scored a winning point. 'By how much?'

'A football field,' Danny muttered as he swapped places with Beau.

'I heard that,' Brooke called out.

'With the same ears that heard the ball whiz past your chest, not your knees as your racket seemed to believe?'

Her eyes narrowed and her chin dropped. 'Oh, now you've gone and done it, Danny boy. This was going to be a fun match. But now the game's well and truly on.'

'Promise?' he asked.

She sauntered down to the front of the court. It seemed her hours of watching tennis on TV had given her some idea of where to stand at least. Her eyes remained dead ahead, though he could tell that every other sense was well and truly trained on him. The toss of her head, the squaring of her shoulders, the swing of her hips, they were all for his benefit.

Okay, so he no longer felt like laughing. Now he was well and truly turned on. After that conversation on the lawn, all that talk of bedrooms, and tapes, and courses and blowing her mind. He wished he had Lleyton Hewitt on the other side of the court so that he could exhaust the tension right out of himself with a proper tennis match.

'Lily, I'm serving to you now,' Beau called out, right leg forward, ball balanced on his racket. 'Go up the back where Mum was before.'

Lily unhooked herself from the net and ran to the back of the court. She held the too-heavy racket over her head and waited with adorable concentration.

Beau took a few moments to centre himself, his young face tempered by such serious preparation. Then he threw the ball and—whack! The kid had style. Danny knew that the best sportsmen were born, not made, and most of them were on their way to proving it already by Beau's age.

The ball bounced and Lily rushed at it, her boa flying, her tutu bouncing. And the ball flew a good metre over her head.

'I've got it,' Brooke said.

She skipped to the back of the court and waited for the ball to bounce against the fence, and then she managed to get her racket under it and hooked it high over the net to Danny's side of the court. It bounced in front of him, once, twice and then dribbled to end up at his feet.

Brooke threw her arms in the air and let out a great whoop of delight. 'Our point!' she cried out.

Danny stared at her, taking in the expanse of slightly rounded stomach revealed as her arms punched the air and her tank top rode a good three inches higher than the belt line of her shorts. There was just enough room between her clothing for a man's hand to fit flush against her skin. His hand. His throat grew tight at the thought.

'Your point according to what, and who?' he growled. 'And are you out of your mind?'

'Findlay family rules.' She swung her racket and sashayed back to the edge of the court. Her mouth kicked up into an utterly sexy smile.

'And what are those?' Danny asked.

She got into position, racket forward, bottom swaying back and forth, saucy grin very much in place and Danny found a sudden need to clear his throat.

'We make them up as we go along,' she said.

Danny turned to his less disquieting partner, who was already waiting to make his next serve. 'Are you listening to this?'

Beau shrugged. 'I don't mind.'

'You don't mind?' Danny repeated. 'The kid doesn't mind. Well, it seems I'm outvoted. The Findlay family rules it is.'

He had a horrible feeling that he was going to lose today. And Danny hated to lose. It had been his formative experience that losing meant tears and dashed hopes and having to move apartments again. He made it his mission never to feel that way again.

Yet somehow, as the game progressed, and the Findlays regularly changed teams between points, and changed sides between shots, and used their hands to hit the ball, and created their own scoring structure, he found that he'd never had more fun losing in his whole life.

Every miss brought forth endearing giggles, and every hit was celebrated with world-championship-level gusto. And the chance to watch Brooke laugh, and live, and smile a smile brimming with confidence and happiness and burgeoning self-belief felt like a whole new kind of victory.

And it was a taste he knew he would never get enough of.

An hour later, after washing off the grime and sweat and dirt and aches that came with an afternoon of chasey, and swings and tennis, Brooke padded down the stairs, rubbing at her wet hair with a towel.

'No, this is Beau,' she heard her son say. His next words were, 'They are both in the shower.' And that had Brooke flying into the kitchen and snatching the phone from his hand.

'Sorry,' she said into the handset. 'I'm here. This is Brooke. How can I help?'

'Brooke Findlay?' a woman on the other end said.

'Yep.' She gave Beau a quick kiss on the top of the head, before he squirmed out of her arms and ran away.

'Calvin Findlay's wife?' the woman said, and this time Brooke felt the hairs on the back of her neck begin to itch.

'Who is this?' she asked.

'Rachel Cross. I am a researcher for *Sports Scene.*'

'*Sports Scene,*' Brooke repeated deadpan, wishing she'd got to the phone first.

'The TV show hosted by Martin Bradshaw—'

Brooke licked her dry lips. 'I know what *Sports Scene* is. Danny is indisposed at the moment, but I can take a message.'

'Still in the shower, is he?' The young woman let that thought float on the air.

'I have no idea,' Brooke returned. She itched to hang up the phone, but the fact that it wasn't her phone just meant that she couldn't.

'Well, actually,' the woman said, 'I'm really glad I got

you. How would you feel about appearing on Thursday night's show?'

'Me? You do realise that I am not, and never have been, a sportswoman. Throw a ball at me and just watch me duck.'

'Oh, I know, but we like to focus on the personal rather than the public face of professional sports. Danny could come on too. In fact the two of you on together would be even better.'

'Well… Rachel, was it?'

'Ya ha.'

'I don't see that happening any time this millennium. Now, if you want to talk to Danny, I suggest you call him at work. But if you call here again while I am under this roof, or if you come within sight of my kids, I will sue you for harassment. Have a good day,' she said sweetly before pressing the disconnect button with such vehemence she bruised her fingertip.

She knew they all knew she was here. She knew they knew that her kids were here too. But now one of *them* knew that she and Danny had taken showers in the middle of the day. At the same time. No matter that she'd joked about it with Danny earlier, she understood how important spin was to these people, and things were fast spinning out of control.

'Did I hear the phone ring?' Danny asked and she leapt a good two inches off the ground.

She turned to find him ambling down the stairs in calf-length khaki cargo pants, a black T-shirt and no shoes. Her gaze travelled upwards from big feet, past a smattering of dark hair covering the calves of a runner. His T-shirt was moulded to the shoulders of a swimmer. He had the soft smile of a guy who had spent ten minutes under steaming hot jets of water, and a face that could stop traffic.

Her heart tripped over itself, her throat turned dry and her cheeks warmed. It had been such a long time since she had these kinds of reactions, maybe she was mistaking things. Mistaking appreciation for affection. Comfort for attraction. History for a connection the depth of which she had never experienced.

Or was that why she was so upset when people intimated things about her and Danny, when Simone teased her, or newspapers printed inflammatory and suggestive articles? Because there was a chance they could be right? But that was insane, wasn't it? The idea that she and Danny Finch could ever, would ever, be anything more than friendly adversaries. There was far too much water under the bridge and they both had far too much to lose.

'Beau is some tennis player,' Danny said, oblivious to the panic pinning her to the spot. 'We should do something about that.'

She clutched the phone tight to her chest. 'We should?'

He ran a hand over his damp hair, creating a mass of sexy spikes, awakening a surplus of long dormant butterflies to fly rampant through her insides.

'It's best to start him on top-notch lessons now. I know a guy who runs a private clinic after school and during holidays. I can give him a call.'

A call. A guy. A private clinic. After the conversation she'd just had, and the reactions she was now having to the man before her, Brooke was struggling to keep up. 'Um, how about I talk to Beau later? See what he thinks. If he wants to keep up the lessons when he changes schools then I'll do what I can.'

Danny glanced at her and all of a sudden his face fell. The soft smile disappeared and his cheeks turned a gorgeous shade of pink. The Danny she knew *wasn't* meant to blush. He was meant to be cool, and aloof, and sharp and unreachable. But the Danny she was coming to know was an entirely different beast.

'That was bloody insensitive of me,' he said. 'I should

have kept my mouth shut and given the lessons to Beau for his birthday, rather than adding more financial pressure.' He ran his hand through his hair again, this time with a clenched arm that had muscles upon muscles, and Brooke found it hard to remember how to breathe.

'But allow me to do this for you,' he said, his golden eyes pleading, apologising, begging her to give into his wishes. 'Please. If it's what he wants, let me find him the best coaching this town has to offer.'

'Danny—'

He placed a hand over his heart and said, 'It is not even in the same ball park as charity. It would be my pleasure.'

Her chest felt so warm and jittery it truly felt as though he'd placed his other hand over her heart. 'Fine,' she said. 'And you can do me a favour in return.' Brooke thrust the phone into his hand. 'Call Emily.'

His beautiful face relapsed into a frown and for a moment she wondered if he had any idea who she was talking about.

'Your girlfriend Emily,' she added.

He took the phone but made no move to press any buttons. Instead he moved a step closer and laid the phone down on the bench. 'And what would you like me to say to her when I call her?'

'Invite her to dinner. Tonight. With Simone and Jerry.'

'May I ask why?'

Good question. One she couldn't scoot around. *Okay, here goes.* 'Some girl from *Sports Scene* just rang and intimated some things that I don't think are worth repeating and I think it would be a good idea for all of us if Emily came here. Tonight. And told a lot of people she was doing so.'

She waited for him to look at her as if she was nuts. He looked at her all right, but as if she was intriguing, engaging and important. Her throat burned with a sudden need to tell him that he was all those things to her as well. Even though he wasn't. He couldn't be. He was just Danny. Her antagonist and her rock. But not her prospective…what? Lover?

Despite their earlier teasing, she hadn't believed for one hot second that a guy like Danny would need classes in that area. Not a guy with lips like his, with hands like his, with eyes that could look at a woman like he did. Her knees melted so suddenly she had to reach out and grab hold of the kitchen bench.

'Okay, then,' he said. 'I'll do that for you. Did she want me to call her back?'

'Who?'

'The girl from *Sports Scene*. Was it Rachel? I've been negotiating a spot to talk about one of my netballers in the next couple of weeks.'

'Ah, yes it was. And no, I don't think that would be a bright idea to call her back right away. Maybe leave it a couple of days. And call from your office.'

His cheek twitched, but he left it at that. Then he sauntered into the kitchen proper to grab an apple from the fruit bowl. As he passed she was hit with a wave of citrus scent so sharp and fresh she actually licked her lips.

She reached out and grabbed the phone which he had left behind and slapped it against his chest.

'Now?' he asked, his voice close, and low and deep, the vibrations rumbling through his chest, into the phone and down her arm.

She nodded. How she would explain herself to the woman when she came to dinner she had no idea. But that was the least of her worries. She needed to put a face to the name, and a personality to the thought. She needed Emily Whatever-her-name-was to be flesh and blood. And lovely. And perfect for Danny.

And she needed to see him look at Emily with even more warmth and care and kindness and interest than he had shown her over the past few days.

He reached up and closed his hand over the phone, and over her hand at the same time. His fingers were deliciously warm. The look in his eyes far too knowing.

She disengaged herself from the phone and from him and all but fled the room.

CHAPTER SEVEN

A KNOCK came at the front door.

'Can you get that?' Danny called out from the kitchen.

Brooke flinched and the acrylic fingernail she was nibbling on tore right off. Oh, well, she'd broken two more while playing outside with the kids and couldn't afford the upkeep anyway. Funny thing was, she found that she didn't much care.

She ran a hand over her loose hair and did as Danny asked. But by the time she reached the front door Beau and Lily were already there.

'Hang on, kids,' she said, but it was too late, Beau had wrenched the door open.

'Oh, hello,' a pretty feminine voice with a soft British accent said.

Brooke came around the corner to find a tall woman with long biscuit-brown waves, a peaches-and-cream complexion and voluptuous curves poured into a mushroom-coloured designer skirt suit. She was lovely, and perfect, and flesh and blood. Yet somehow it didn't make Brooke feel as instantly improved as she had hoped it would.

'Who are you?' Lily asked.

'Lily,' Brooke said, placing herself in front of her kids. 'Sorry. Hi, I'm Brooke. You must be Emily.'

The woman smiled and held out a long thin hand, the thumb adorned with gold. So she was lovely and cool to boot. 'That I am,' she said.

Brooke shook her hand.

'And this must be Beau and Lily.' Emily leant over, placing her hands on her lean thighs. 'Aren't you both just too adorable.'

Lily jumped up and down and flapped her feather boa and took the praise while Beau sneaked behind Brooke's denim-clad legs.

'Come on in,' Brooke said, running a comforting hand across Beau's forehead. 'Danny's in the kitchen. I'm sure he'll be just thrilled to see you. He's talked of little else since…well, this afternoon when he called. I'm afraid we've been monopolising his time these last few days, so I apologise for that too.'

Okay, so she was blathering. And Emily was smiling kindly, which only made it worse.

'Why don't you head on through to Danny and we'll go out and wait for my sister to arrive,' Brooke finished, needing to take a deep breath once she was done.

Beau sneaked through a gap and ran out into the front yard. Not to be left out, Lily followed. A security light switched on so at least Brooke could see them. But it also left her alone with the lovely Emily. Danny's girl. Danny's item. The last woman Danny would ever kiss?

Emily smiled down at her, far too tall for comfort in her high heels. Brooke tried to smile back, but she suddenly felt underdressed in her faded jeans and pink floral peasant blouse. 'So I'll go that way and…'

Emily pointed into the house. 'And I'll go that way.'

Brooke's bare feet squeaked on the polished wood floor as she headed out the front door, while Emily's high heels made soft feminine clacking noises behind her.

Brooke glanced back, just the once. She should have been delighted, happy her friend had found such a lovely woman. And happy for her own peace of mind that he had someone he could take out on the town to take the heat off her. But so far she felt strangely unconvinced.

A pair of wavering headlights flickered through the tree trunks. Brooke slid her feet into a pair of Danny's huge flip-flops at the front door and headed out on to the gravel drive, knowing with Simone on her way she had far more things to worry about than long legs and long hair and sophistication beyond her means.

'Lily!' Simone called out, hopping out of the car before it had fully stopped.

'Auntie Simoooone,' Lily cried, throwing herself into her aunt's arms. She giggled like crazy as Simone covered her with kisses.

'And how's my favourite little heartbreaker?' Simone asked. Beau batted his dark eyelashes, making his big blue eyes gleam.

'You little flirt,' Simone said, squishing his cheeks until his lips pouted like a fish. 'You couldn't go ten feet in your pram without being stopped by women gooing and fawning over you. I guess that ran in the family.'

Simone let go of Beau, slid Lily back to the ground and gave Brooke a kiss on the cheek.

'Go wash up and then you can say your goodnights,' Brooke said.

Beau moaned, as though she was the hardest mother in the whole world. But they did as they were told, running across the gravel like the wind was at their heels.

'He gets better-looking every day, that kid,' Simone said, as she slipped an arm through Brooke's. She watched Beau run inside with something akin to wistfulness, though Brooke knew that Simone was as wistful as a train lamenting passing a pretty lake without slowing to take a better look.

'Don't tell him that. Hey, Jerry,' she threw over her shoulder as Simone's boyfriend slowly dragged his lethargic form out of the car.

'Hey, Findlay,' he said, reaching into the back seat for a cooler containing at least four bottles of wine.

'How's the home brew coming along?'

He took one last puff on a cigarette, knowing he wouldn't get a look at another while her kids were about. 'I've moved into making my own petrol now.'

'Excellent.'

Simone rolled her eyes. 'Is someone else here?' She stared at the sleek red sports car they passed in the driveway.

'A friend of Danny's,' Brooke said.

'Male?'

'Female. Her name is Emily. They are an item.'

Simone's right eyebrow disappeared beneath her severe dark fringe. 'Well, well, well, this is going to be the funnest night I've had in a long while.'

Brooke grimaced. 'Let's just try for pleasant and leave fun for another time, okay?'

By nine o'clock Danny was in need of a Scotch.

Even though, by and large, considering he had innocently invited Brooke's prickly sister, and Brooke had quite purposely invited his supposed girlfriend, and it could have been a disaster, everything had gone swimmingly. Or as swimmingly as he could have hoped.

As usual Simone was wily and divisive, but at least she didn't stomp on any one person's feelings more than any other.

Jerry drank only soft drinks and managed to spill less food down his front than usual. And the kids only sneaked downstairs twice before finally succumbing to sleep in their own beds.

Thank goodness Emily smiled prettily and laughed melodiously and generally kept the conversation rocketing as he was too busy trying to figure out why Simone smiled at him like the cat who'd got the cream, and Brooke spent a great deal of time topping up her wineglass or staring at her plate.

Realising a quick trip to the den for a nip wasn't really in order, Danny decided to go for some fresh air instead. He stood and began to clear. As she had done the past couple of nights, Brooke did the same.

Until Emily placed a hand over Brooke's and said, 'Sit. I insist.'

Brooke opened her mouth to negotiate, but then she stopped. Her cheeks went pink. And she slowly sat back down in her chair.

Danny waited until Emily followed him into the kitchen before asking, 'Was it absolutely necessary for you to encourage Simone the stirrer in there when she got talking about that stupid survey?'

'I read that survey she was talking about.' Emily grinned and gave him a little shove with her hip as she ended up in front of the sink. 'Apparently eighty per cent of men do cheat.'

'Not apt, considering the company,' he said. 'And that figure is feminist claptrap.'

'So you've never gone there?' Emily asked. 'A big strapping gorgeous thing like you. Melting women galore at balls and parties. And not to mention all those cheerleaders and beach volleyball gals who cross your path. Phew! The temptation.'

'Nevertheless,' he growled, leaning against the bench and crossing his arms, 'I am not a percentile.'

Emily turned on the hot water tap and began to rinse off

the dinner plates. 'Though by cheating I don't just mean stolen kisses or quickies behind the grandstand. I mean physically *or* emotionally.'

'Emotionally?' Danny repeated. 'What chick-centric magazine did you say started this stimulating exploration of sexual politics?'

Emily turned off the tap. 'Classic avoidance technique, my friend. Just tell me, for the sake of my own little poll, have you ever pictured yourself in one woman's arms while making love to another? Did you ever close your eyes and pretend I was somebody else?'

Danny wished Simone was there with him now so he could wring her skinny neck for starting this in the first place. Then he wanted to wring Brooke's neck for insisting he invite Emily along to enjoy the show. He knew he'd never live this down.

'Don't look at me like that, Danny,' Emily said, laughing so hard she had to grab his arm to keep upright. 'I was only kidding. We all know what a good boy you are. The last of the truly honourable men.'

Danny let out a long slow breath. 'Remind me to never feed any of you lamb chops again. It sent you all into the twilight zone.'

Emily grinned as she swiped a last glob of clotted cream off a dessert plate and sucked it into her mouth. 'That's the great thing about dinner parties. All that wine and shifting conversation and low lighting. It brings out the most illuminating conversations.'

Danny glanced back to the swinging door. He for one was glad she hadn't asked such questions ten minutes beforehand. It would have either showed him up as a rogue or a liar. Neither of which made him feel particularly honourable in that moment.

'Are you nervous the natives are getting restless in there

without us?' Emily asked, following the direction of his gaze with her own. 'Or would you have preferred I let Mrs Findlay play hostess? I just figured if that was your plan you should have seated her at the foot of the table.'

'I'd be more happy if you continued rinsing or got out of the way so I can do it.'

Emily moved a metre sideways and he continued the chore in her stead, the steam billowing out of the sink mirroring his mood precisely.

'So whose decision was it to put me at the foot of the table?' she asked.

'Does that matter?'

Emily chuckled. 'Of course it does. If it was your choice then that means you are sending a message to those at the table that I'm your gal. But if it was *her* choice, then you ought to think long and hard about what that might mean.'

Danny rinsed the last plate and stacked it on the sink, then turned off the tap. 'It was hers,' he admitted.

'Well, then, my friend, either that means that she is telling you to back off, or she is finding it very hard to do the same.'

Danny blew out a long hard puff of air, rested his palms against the bench and looked to the ceiling for inspiration, but all he saw was a water stain that would need seeing to. 'No chance you want to go back out there and ask which?'

Emily laughed and patted him on the arm. 'You got it in one, sweetheart. No chance.' She kissed him on the cheek, grinned again, then headed back to the dining room.

He reached up and ran a finger over the spot where she had kissed him. It left no tingle, no warmth; it had felt as sexy as if he'd been kissed by his great-aunt.

He was infinitely glad the two of them had remained friends after their disastrous attempt at dating a few years before. Emily was a great support, an excellent eye for young football talent and a lively dinner companion.

But she was not, and never would be, the 'item' he had led Brooke to believe she could be.

An hour later Emily had said her goodbyes and gone home.

Jerry and Danny were outside smoking a couple of Danny's cigars and talking sports. Simone and Brooke had gone upstairs to peek in on the kids and had ended up in Brooke's bedroom.

Simone let herself fall until she lay spreadeagled on Brooke's massive borrowed bed. 'How much money do you think you need to start over?'

'Enough to feed and clothe my kids. A roof over our heads. As good a school as I can afford. Day care for Lily so I can get a job. And now Danny is making noises about getting Beau into top-flight tennis lessons. A zillion bucks ought to do it.' Brooke gave in and slumped back on to the bed so that she lay beside her sister. 'Why? You got that kind of money lying around?'

'Not quite a zillion,' Simone said. 'But a few thousand. Though we were thinking of putting a down payment on a trip to the moon. Or blowing it all on red at the casino. But if you need me to help release the pressure of having to sort it out with Mr Hotstuff breathing down your neck and confusing the issue then it's yours.'

Brooke turned her head sideways, then had to lift her head to push her hair to the other side lest she swallow a mouthful. 'Mr Hotstuff is breathing nowhere near my neck. He is simply being an unbelievably good friend. And at the moment everything is comfortable, so please don't do or say or even think anything to make it otherwise. But I'll think about your offer. Seriously. Okay? Happy now?'

Simone didn't pretend not to understand her. 'I'm happy that you're happy. And that Danny's happy.'

'He's not happy. He's just—'

'Your knight in shining armour.'

Brooke looked up at the ceiling. 'Emily's pretty fabulous, don't you think?'

Simone screwed up her nose. 'I guess. If you like leggy women with big boobs.'

'Well, that's never been *my* type…'

'She's a decoy anyway, you know.'

Brooke knew. She had known the moment she'd seen them together. The moment Emily had touched Danny on the arm and he hadn't even seemed to notice. He noticed every single time she touched him. And she noticed every single time he touched her. But she was not going to tell her sister that.

Simone made kissy noises with her mouth as she shifted and stared at the ceiling too. 'I hit on him once, you know.'

'You did not!' Brooke said, lifting her torso and leaning on her hand.

'Mmm-hmm. Waaaay back at the beginning. At that barbecue Cal threw to "bring the clans together".'

'What happened?'

'Our eyes met across a crowded room…'

Brooke feigned a punch at Simone's arm and she flinched.

'Okay! Sorry. Well, as I remember it, your Danny was working the barbecue, which is, of course, always the job of the alpha male.'

Brooke slid down again until she was facing upwards as well, her head tucked into her big sister's shoulder. It reminded her of nights just after their parents died, when Simone had let her sleep in her bed. They would leave the curtains open and, lit by moonlight, would reminisce for hours. It had been nice for a bit. Before things had seemed to shift overnight and Simone had begun to blame her for everything and she'd begun to believe it.

'Danny was talking to a couple of other guys, and taking his barbecuing job very seriously. His brow was furrowed, his mouth stern, his back straight. And, boy, oh, boy, was he the most gorgeous thing I had ever laid eyes on.'

Brooke blinked, thinking back to that day for what must have been the umpteenth time that week. She remembered most the way his eyes had never roved when he'd been talking to someone, he'd never looked out over the crowd to see who else had arrived. He'd just been content to be in the moment, and that was something she'd never considered possible before. She'd spent far too many years looking backwards and forward and back again that she'd felt as if she had permanent whiplash.

'Then what?' Brooke asked, her voice soft.

'Then, the minute he was free, I made my move. I fluffed my hair, pumped up my boobs and sauntered on over with my best "if you want me I'm yours" expression. He was polite, he listened, but still I knew that I wasn't the most gorgeous thing he'd ever laid eyes on.'

Simone gave a great sigh.

'Your Danny must have broken half a dozen hearts that day. I watched as one girl after another smiled, simpered, laughed, touched his arm and slipped him their phone number. All the while he remained untouched.'

Silence stretched as Simone let her words hang on the air like gathering clouds.

'He's not my Danny,' Brooke whispered.

'No? Then how come the only time I saw his expression

change, the only time I saw him smile, and laugh, and lean in, and reach back that day was when he was talking to you. If he's not your Danny, then he'd damn sure like to be.'

'Don't be ridiculous. Danny could have any woman he wants.'

'Well, my sweet young sister, he wants you. Has wanted you for as long as I've known him. And now, finally, after pining after you for eight years, he has a chance. Whether or not he would ever admit it to himself, he has brought you here not out of any sense of altruism but because he simply couldn't help it. The question of the day is, does he have as big a chance as he would like?'

Simone turned her head to look at Brooke, but Brooke kept her eyes locked on to the ceiling. The truth was he did have a chance. She'd always felt a connection with him. *Always.* Something sure and strong and volatile and challenging and frustrating that went beyond pretty words and secret glances. Something deeper. For he was sensitive, smart and easily the sexiest man to ever walk the planet.

She breathed in through her nose and let the air out in a long skinny stream through her front teeth. 'I'm a bad person.'

Simone choked out a laugh. 'And why is that?'

'What if you're right? What if I have been carrying on some kind of tragic unspoken love affair the whole time I was married to Cal? Just like you intimated so bloody obviously at dinner. What if I have been emotionally unfaithful for years? Isn't that as bad as if I'd thrown myself at Danny?'

'Brooke, Brooke, Brooke. You think far too much. Always have. Just accept things as they are for once and get on with it. Stop trying to overanalyse every damn thing.'

'But—'

'But nothing. You're not a bad person. You were far too

good for Cal, but while you were with him you only ever had eyes for him. Don't you think if I had seen a crack I would have shoved in a wedge and pushed for all I was worth to get you away from him? You're insecure, and a little bit of a martyr. But you're also the least bad person I know.'

Brooke blinked. Wow. Maybe they should drink too much white wine together more often.

'So what are you going to do about it?' Simone asked.

Brooke dragged her woozy bones upright and ran both hands hard over her face. 'Nothing, of course.'

'Excellent,' Simone said, her voice ripe with sarcasm. 'Especially since Danny is as noble as you are. The two of you will go on circling one another and pretending nothing is going on and then, when you are old and grey and prostrate on your deathbed, while he holds a cool towel to your forehead day in and day out, then you can finally admit that you are mad about him.'

'Findlay? Simone?' Jerry's voice called from somewhere down the hall and Brooke flinched so hard she pulled a muscle in her calf.

'In here!' Simone called out, not moving an inch from her comfy spot.

Jerry pushed the bedroom door open and looked from one sister to the other. They must have looked a sight as his brow knitted and he whispered, 'Am I interrupting?'

'Yes, thank God,' Brooke said.

And then Danny's face appeared around the door. 'We thought the two of you might have been kidnapped by aliens,' he said.

'Not me,' Brooke said, hoping that he had no idea how fast her heart had suddenly started beating the moment he had shown his face, 'but I've had doubts about this one for years.'

'Come on in, Jerry, you have to feel this bed,' Simone said. 'This is truly the mattress of the gods.'

Jerry grinned then strolled over and sat on a patch of bed, bouncing up and down on a corner and squeezing the mattress with both hands. With every bounce down Brooke bounced up.

'I don't remember sending out invites to a slumber party,' she said.

'Coming, Danny?' Simone bellowed, shifting her bottom sideways to leave room. 'We're all family here. There's plenty of room.'

Thankfully Danny stayed in the doorway, leaning his long form against the doorjamb. Four in the bed would have had her swearing off white wine for good.

'Thanks for the offer,' he said, 'but I have bounced on that bed before.' And then his glinting gaze shifted sideways. To Brooke. His smile changed. Softened. Became gentle. She felt aglow and as if she wanted to throw up all at once.

'Besides,' he said, 'I would never enter a woman's bedroom without her express permission.'

'Now, if that's not angling for an invitation then I don't know what is.' Simone's head rolled sideways so that she could grin up at Brooke. A couple of Groucho Marx eyebrow raises were enough for Brooke to leap off the bed and clap her hands.

'Okay, you lot,' Brooke said. 'Party's over. Out. Now.'

Simone groaned and uncurled herself from the bed and leant on Jerry. 'You're just too good to be true, aren't you, Mr Finch?' she said, pinching Danny on the cheek as she slipped out the door.

'Don't believe it for a second,' he said.

'Nice mattress,' Jerry said as he followed.

'I've always thought so.'

'I'm not the one who invited them,' Brooke added as she

turned off the light behind her and made to slide past, but Danny's hand snaked out and clasped around the doorframe, blocking her path.

She watched helplessly as Simone and Jerry disappeared around the corner and their clomping footsteps echoed down the stairs.

'Is everything okay?' he asked, his voice deep and gentle in the darkness.

'Sure. Why wouldn't it be?'

'You look…flushed. I thought she might have said something to upset you. Again.'

Brooke laughed, and willed the blood to stop flowing to her cheeks. 'If she didn't already have a job, she could list that as her profession. But I'm fine. She's fine. She said nothing new. And, even if she did, I can take it.'

His eyes narrowed, piercing her. She did her best to block him from seeing too deeply inside her, to see how much his presence affected her. To block out the sensation of his large form leaning into her, electricity shooting up her arm from where his arm brushed hers, his tangy scent curling about her, drawing her in, making her want to lean and shift and melt against him and let him stand up for her always.

Finally he let her go, his fingers sliding away from the doorway with such lack of pace it felt so much as if he was loath to let her go. As such she stayed, attached to him still by far more than touch. By mottled history, and brand-new attraction, and the sheer force of his personality.

He drew in a long slow breath and she felt his chest expand, shifting the air around her, making her feel almost claustrophobic in their now customary-purposeful-accidental meeting spot in the doorway.

'I'd better check they have made it out the front door,' she said. 'Knowing my luck, they'll accidentally fall in the pool or, worse, asleep in the den, and then we'll never see the back of them.'

Danny smiled, barely, but it was enough. Warmth eased through her at his glance, at the growing desire to prolong this moment, this night, and every night that she spent under his roof.

When he moved away and let her pass, she didn't sprint down the hall, but it was near enough. As such she made it to the front door to see off their guests a good half minute before Danny joined them.

'You have to find out where he bought his sheets,' Simone said as she leaned in for a last goodbye kiss. 'They are pure heaven.'

'Sure,' Brooke said, 'I'll do that.'

'Take care, you two,' Simone said, and Brooke knew Danny was behind her. His familiar scent caught on a breeze and cocooned her.

Simone gave the two of them one last smile, brimming with understanding. Not for the first time, Brooke wished she was an only child. She spun her sister around and gave her a shove. 'Goodbye, Simone.'

'Ta ta!' she said and turned and jogged down the front steps to Jerry's waiting car.

'Well, that was fun,' Brooke said as she closed the door.

'Mmm,' he said, 'let's do it all again soon. We make quite a party. You, me, your crazy sister, her odd friend.'

'And Emily,' she added. 'We can't forget her.'

'No,' Danny said, 'it seems we can't.'

Before he offered her a nightcap that she couldn't refuse, Brooke eased around him and towards the stairs. It wasn't likely she would get to sleep for a good while with all the thoughts and feelings buzzing through her, but she knew it was best if she was thinking and feeling those things without this particular distraction in the room with her.

'Goodnight, Danny.'

'See you in the morning when the sun comes up.'

She laughed. Softly. As though the night required gentle peace. Then turned and jogged upstairs to her bed. A bed he had made, covered in sheets he had bought.

Pure heaven, Simone had said. But Brooke wasn't sure she was equipped to deal with pure heaven if it ever came her way.

CHAPTER EIGHT

SEVERAL days later Beau came down the stairs, ready for his first day at the local state school. His new school uniform, consisting of a red tartan shirt and khaki shorts, was at least a size too big, but Danny knew better than to say so.

'I look stupid,' Beau said, tugging at his shirt and accidentally untucking the left side. Danny looked around for Brooke, but she was in the middle of trying to locate Lily's feather boa, which had gone missing at some stage that morning, sending Lily into an out-and-out tantrum.

Beau stopped at the bottom of the stairs and sniffed. Danny wondered if he had been crying. His heart thumped hard against his ribs as memories came crowding in on him.

'Come here,' he said, his voice croaky.

Beau did as he was told, dragging his feet down the last two steps until he stood looking up at Danny, big blue eyes so like Cal's but with none of the snake-charmer lurking beneath.

Danny bent down to his haunches and tucked Beau's shirt back in. Beau just stood there and took it, rocking on his feet like a rag doll. Up close he smelled of new cotton and cornflakes. Up close Danny could see the red in his eyes.

Beau sniffed again and didn't even try to hide it. Danny

ached to haul him into his arms and hug him. Just hug him. To tell him he knew how he felt. That he had seen his own mother try to find the way to a new life with a new man and had seen it crash and burn time and again, had watched his mother collapse further in on herself with every new failure while she'd tried to stay strong and perky for his sake alone. And that he would never let that happen to Brooke.

But he was scared that if he tried it, Beau might pull away. He might flinch and struggle and hate him for simply being a man who was not his father. And he wouldn't blame the kid if he did. So instead he just smiled and reached out and ruffled his hair. 'I have a present for you,' he said.

'What for?' Beau asked, pushing his glasses higher on his nose.

'Starting a new school. Didn't you know that every kid gets a special present on their first day? It's one of the million cool things about starting a new school.'

Beau's mouth pursed as though he didn't quite believe he could be that lucky. Then he looked up and over Danny's shoulder and he realised Brooke was there.

'What's the present?' Beau asked before the chance was snatched away.

Danny felt Brooke watching him. He felt her questioning glare at the back of his neck. He hadn't asked her permission before getting a gift for Beau and, well, he didn't really want her permission. This was about him and the kid. It was a guy thing. And she could just lump it.

'I have managed to beg, borrow and call in about a dozen favours in order to get four tickets to…guess what?'

Beau licked his lips, his eyes getting wider as he imagined what the 'guess what' could possibly be.

Danny pulled four small rectangles of cardboard from behind his back and used them to scratch his chin. 'Tickets to the AFL footy grand final at the end of this month.'

Beau gawped. His mouth dropped open. And his eyes all but popped out of his head. 'Are you serious?'

'I am. You, your mum and sister can come with me. With those tickets you can go anywhere you want. You'll sit in the Collingwood family seats with all the players' kids, and if they make the grand final you can come back into the rooms after the game.'

He handed the tickets to Beau who held on to them as though they were made of butterfly wings.

'Can I take these to school?' For this he looked up at his mum, which meant that Danny was forced to as well.

He stood, his thirty-three-year-old knees creaking, and turned to face her. She had Lily, now calm and smiling, with her feather boa wrapped about the two of them so one couldn't move without the other.

Brooke didn't look entirely happy. But that wasn't why his chest felt as if a steel band had been tightened around it. She looked utterly chaotic. Her hair was a shaggy mess, her cheeks were pink and her chest rose and fell as though she'd been running for ten minutes straight, which she likely had. She looked so beautiful, and so right just being there in his home every morning, it hurt him to breathe.

'Mum, can I take these to school?' Beau asked again, all but skipping over to show her the tickets. 'I promise I won't bend them or lose them.'

'I guess that's up to Danny,' she said, her voice husky, her eyes never leaving his.

'They're yours, Beau,' he said, though he kept his gaze on Brooke. 'Yours to do with as you please. So long as you remember that I have entrusted you with something precious. And when you have something precious under your care you can't take such an honour lightly.'

'Okay, I promise,' Beau said, sliding the tickets into a pocket of his backpack.

Brooke blinked. She was too far away for Danny to see if the weight of his words reached her. If she had any idea that he was talking about himself. And about her.

And then, just as he thought his confession had fallen on deaf ears, she smiled. It was barely there. More of a softening of the eyes, and a widening of the mouth, and a general lovely shimmer that surrounded her, creating a swell of such warmth inside him that he didn't want to ever forget what that felt like.

For that feeling, that sense of rightness, of accomplishment, of connection, made the years of holding back, of not settling for anything less, all worth it. The bright light of possibility raged within him, unstopped, illuminating all the deep dark hurt places inside him until he felt…happy.

'Right. Now that's all settled,' Brooke said, breaking the spell and turning away, 'let's get this show on the road.'

She uncurled herself from the boa's grasp, collected Lily's Wiggles overnight bag from near the front door and followed her hyperactive daughter and his equally delighted dog outside. This could go on forever, Danny thought, the happy places inside him continuing to swell. Beau slid his hand inside Danny's and held on tight all the way. If they all just chose to forget about how they got here, maybe, perhaps, things could simply stay as they were.

'What are the other cool things?' Beau asked as they locked up the front door.

Danny pocketed his keys, then leaned in and whispered, 'The teachers have no idea what mark you got in your last spelling test.'

At that Beau smiled. A smile that tied them together in the sharing of secret men's business.

And then to the car, and Danny was mighty glad nobody was close enough to see the very unmanly gleam in his eyes.

Danny and Brooke dropped Beau at school.

He looked so small, his huge backpack almost as big as him. But at least here he would be at a school far enough away from Melbourne to give him anonymity, and big enough to give him access to an excellent curriculum and a great sporting programme. Danny had quietly done his own research and made sure of that. He had also even more quietly revelled in the knowledge that with Beau starting school in Emerald, it meant that even if and when Brooke moved out she planned to stay close.

Miss Chapman, Beau's pretty young teacher, took him in hand and was babbling away excitedly as she guided him up the wide grey front steps. A little red-headed girl, jealous of the attention, ran up and took her other hand.

'She's cute,' Danny said, hoping to get a rise out of Brooke, who hadn't said boo to him all morning. Since the smile that had sent him over the moon, she seemed to have shrunk back inside herself on the drive until she was almost unreachable.

His ploy worked. She turned and glared at him. 'It's the freckles.'

His cheek twitched. 'I meant the taller one.'

'What a shock. I can't see a wedding ring from here. Do you want me to find out her phone number?'

He said, 'Not my type.'

'Why not? And don't tell me it's because of Emily.'

Okay. So it seemed she had seen through that ruse quick smart. 'It's not,' he admitted.

She blinked a good half-dozen times, letting that info sink in before glaring out the window instead. 'Then what? You can't tell me you don't like brunettes—I known you've dated half a dozen at least. And she liked you. I saw her batting her lashes at you when she showed us around the classrooms last week. That's always a turn on for a guy, right? If you know you're in with a chance, that's half the work done for you.'

She was in some mood. She had been since Lily's outburst that morning. Maybe even before that. Hell, she'd been running hot and cold with him since dinner with her sister a week before.

'It has nothing to do with her hair colour,' he said, willing her to look his way, but she absolutely refused.

'Fine,' she said, crossing her arms and staring out the window some more. 'I don't know why I bother.'

'Neither do I,' he shot back. Though he was beginning to have a fair idea. He'd been in the doorway with her the night of the dinner party. And a dozen more times since. He'd felt the air shift and move and warm and whisper from her skin to his. He'd seen her watching him, brow furrowed, thoughts taking her somewhere uncertain and untested. He knew she wasn't as immune to him as she was making out.

She waved out the window. Beau waved back. Then he pushed his glasses higher on his nose and walked inside.

Before pulling away from the kerb Danny checked Lily and Buckley were still happy in the back seat. They were—snuggled together, the big chocolate Lab and the small blonde girl.

It was so sweet a picture it actually moved him. And he was rarely moved. When his footy team won a big game, or he posted his first million-dollar profit, sure. But today he had found himself moved by Beau's hand in his and by a small blonde moppet with ringlets clinging tight to his dog as if they were best friends.

He was becoming soft. There was no doubt about it. And no matter what was—or wasn't—going on with Brooke, he certainly could not afford to go soft. There were too many people counting on him to be hard. And sharp. As he always had been.

He squeezed the steering wheel tight until it burned against his palms, looked over his shoulder and pulled out on to the quiet country road and headed towards Melbourne.

It took a good fifteen minutes for Brooke to pipe up again. And, by the tone in her voice, he could tell she had been stewing the whole time. 'You can't keep up with the gifts, Danny. That's not the way to win the kids over.'

'Who says I'm trying to win anybody over?' He shot her a sideways glance to find she was staring dead ahead. The last strains of the warm and fuzzy feelings drifted away like white clouds before a storm.

Stubborn mule of a woman, he thought, clutching to the steering wheel more tightly. If he didn't know better, he would have thought she was trying to pick a fight. Trying to breed hostility between them.

'So gifts aren't the key,' he shot back. 'Or knowing his favourite film. Or losing at tennis to keep him happy. Funny, he seemed pretty stoked with each and every effort.'

She turned to him, her right cheek sucked deep into her mouth as she worried it. 'You're only setting him up for a fall, Danny. If he gets everything his way, he'll only come to expect it. To think it's owed to him.'

Like Cal. She didn't say the words, yet they hung in the air between them. Hell, they more than hung, they dropped like an iron curtain, keeping the two of them determinedly on two sides of the damn thing.

'Fine,' he said, giving in and letting good healthy antipathy wash over his skin until he was soaking in it. 'Whatever you say.'

As soon as Danny pulled up in front of the beach-front hotel in St Kilda, but before the wheels had even come to a full halt, Brooke had her seat belt unbuckled and was out of the car. She couldn't handle being in the car with him a second longer. All that stifling hot air and antagonism was too much to bear.

Even though being back in Melbourne for the first time in days felt strange. She flicked quick glances over her shoulders to make sure there were no hidden cameras. A flash of light made her jump, but it was just sun glinting off the side mirror.

Get a grip, she told herself before opening the back door, careful not to let Buckley out, which was difficult considering Lily had her arms wrapped about his fluffy neck. 'Let go, honey,' she said.

'He's coming with me.'

'Not today. Danny needs him to help at work.'

'Hey, kiddo,' Simone said from behind her.

At that Lily let go, tumbling out of the car and into her aunt's arms. Brooke slammed the door shut but not before she got an arm's length of slobber.

'Are you sure this is a good time to take them?' Brooke asked.

Simone hitched Lily higher on to her hip. 'Don't panic. It's ideal. I won my big case and I've taken a couple of days in lieu before I get tied down with another. And we looove this hotel, don't we, munchkin?'

'Can we go in the pool? I brought my swimmers,' Lily said, lifting up her skirt to show off her bathing suit.

'Course we can,' Simone said.

'I can still pick Beau up from school, you know,' Brooke offered.

Simone shook her head. 'We've been looking forward to this little holiday for days. I've promised him gelato and kicking footy on the beach tonight. He'll be fine.'

Brooke nodded. She knew it to be true. Even though it niggled that Simone had never been able to treat her with the same respect and love when she'd been a kid. She *understood* why. Simone had been eighteen—on the verge of the greatest time of her life—when she'd been stuck with a thirteen-year-old kid. But it still niggled.

Brooke hopped back in the car and wound the window open.

'So you're job hunting today?' Simone asked.

'Yep. Danny's going to set me up in a quiet office at Good Sports with a computer and a week's worth of newspapers so I can apply for a thousand jobs, none of which I will be in the least bit qualified for.'

'Excellent,' Simone said, grinning. She leant over to peer into the window. 'Hey, Danny. Hey...dog.'

'His name's Buckley,' Danny said, leaning closer to Brooke to see Simone. Danny's scent, his delicious scent, wafted past her nose and she clenched her teeth to stop herself from breathing it in. From letting it negate the vigorous head of steam she had spent days cultivating in order to keep him at a necessary arm's length.

'Whatever,' Simone shot back with a smile. 'You two kids have fun today.' She hitched Lily on to her hip and they raced inside the boutique hotel, ready for a couple of days of the best St Kilda had to offer—theme park rides, ice cream and the beach.

'So now it's just you and me,' Danny said, still so close she felt his breath tickling at her hair. His tone was sarcastic, as though he knew just how tenuous her bad mood really was. And the precarious reason behind it.

'Let's get it over and done with then, shall we?' she said, shuffling her backside and buckling up.

His laughter echoed through the car and, no matter how much she tried not to, those seven words, 'So now it's just you and me' rang through her head all the way to his office like some kind of half threat, half delectable promise.

Once inside the Good Sports Agency building Brooke held on to Buckley's collar to stop him from disappearing.

'It's okay,' Danny said, checking messages on his mobile as he hopped into the lift. 'He knows where we're going. And he knows that Lucille will slip him a secret doughnut or two when we get there.'

'Did you really need to bring the dog?' she asked, easing up but letting her hand hover near. She couldn't help herself. She was a mother. The need to protect her over-active charges and to protect others from them came naturally.

'He's fine. He sleeps under my desk and wanders around for a chat every now and then. The staff love it and I don't much like leaving him home alone anyway.'

Of course you don't, Brooke thought, the words rising inside her like a sudden lava flow, burning her throat. For that made Danny soft-hearted. Just another piece to add to the ever widening fabric of his character. A character she was becoming attached to. Profoundly.

In the small enclosed space of the lift she could feel him, smell him, sense him. Her whole body thrummed just from being in such close proximity to him. She was in huge trouble.

For what if something happened, and it didn't work out? What if one day this attraction had the better of her and they kissed and it was awful? What if they went further and found they simply had no sexual chemistry? Or worse, what if their chemistry was as all-comsuming as she imagined it might be? What if she fell harder still, and only then he discovered she wasn't enough for him? And then what if he strayed…?

The lift doors opened, Buckley took off down the hall, and Brooke shot out, gulping in great wads of cool air-conditioned air. She decided that living a life without all-consuming anything wasn't such a bad thing after all. Cut out the heady highs and you also cut out the debilitating lows. And she'd had lows enough.

Danny's mobile rang. He checked the screen. It was Gordon Rose, the super coach. He couldn't leave the guy hanging again. But he didn't want to leave Brooke hanging either. Especially when she was acting as nervous as a cat on a hot tin roof and Lucille was nowhere to be seen.

'I'll be quick,' he promised and meant it. He answered the phone. 'Gordon. You're back?'

The landline began to ring that instant. As Danny listened with one ear to Gordon rant on about his undying love for the team he currently coached, and that he might simply stay put, Danny waited for Lucille to appear. But, alas, she did not.

He looked to Brooke, who smiled thinly at him, then motioned to the phone. He shook his head. The machine could get it. Not ideal, but it would do.

She nodded. Then pulled her handbag tighter to her chest and rocked on her heels.

Gordon was dropping out, so Danny moved to the wall-high window overlooking glorious St Kilda beach, just like the one in his office, and held a finger to his ear.

The landline stopped ringing. He turned back to see that Brooke had moved behind the desk and was in the process of picking up the phone. And he was too late to stop her.

'Good Sports Agency,' she said, waving a hand at Danny when he made to protest. She sat in Lucille's chair, back straight, knees together, handbag still tucked tight under her arm. She listened carefully, his eyebrows lifting ever skyward as the caller obviously gave her a verbal spray that was not sitting well. *Oh, God*, he thought, *let it be a wrong number.*

'Well, Derek, I would like nothing better than to get him for you *this instant*—' She rolled her eyes his way, and the conciliatory move gave him such a kick of adrenalin he had to ask Gordon to repeat himself. 'But Danny's tied up at the moment. I can get him to call you back—'

She was obviously cut off midstream. Her cheeks turned a truly gorgeous shade of pink and Danny could only imagine the tirade she was on the losing end of. For the Derek in question was no doubt Derek Johnson, the long-haired, long-winded kid who looked likely to become the number one pick in the Aussie Rules pre-season draft. Danny wanted him. And he had every intention of getting him. But right now the kid was in the process of butting heads with Brooke, a woman who had been in a mood and a half for a week. And there was nothing he could do to put a stop to it.

He moved back into the room, losing Gordon for a few moments into the process, and looked down the hall, but Lucille was still not in sight.

Suddenly Brooke's eyebrows lowered, she leant back in the chair and placed a relaxed arm over the armrest, her face coming over all beatific. *No. No. No.* He knew that look. When she looked that calm it was worse than when she was dead angry. Derek was about to get an earful. If she lost it with him, the kid would run. And Danny wouldn't blame him.

'Gordon,' Danny said. 'Gordon, you're breaking up and I

can't hear you properly, mate. Give me a couple of minutes and I'll try you again from a landline.'

But by the time he hung up it was too late.

'Derek,' Brooke said, and Danny held his breath. 'Take a breath. Right…now…' She waited. 'Okay. That's better. Now, listen up. Do you really think I would tell you a tale about Danny's whereabouts for my own amusement?'

He walked over to the desk and curled his fingers around the edge, willing her to play nice. She blinked prettily up at him as Derek gave his answer. And then she smiled, all sparkling green eyes and rounded cheeks. Danny's chest loosened up a very little. A smile was good, right? Hell, a smile like that was better than good.

'That's right,' she said. 'Our Danny is a busy boy. Super agents tend to be busy boys. And the last thing we want to do is work him into an early grave. For then where would young men like you be without him on your side?'

Again she waited.

'Beautiful,' she said, leaning forward and grabbing a pen and scribbling down a message. He only hoped it didn't say, Tell Danny to go screw himself.

'I'll pass that on post-haste.' She paused again, cocked her head and smiled. It was such a smile he knew the kid would feel it down the phone line. 'It means quick as I can, okay, Derek? Ciao for now.'

And then she hung up. She rested her elbows on the desk and smiled up at him and said, 'Finished your phone call?'

It was his turn to blink. 'Not quite. What's the message?'

She looked down at the notepaper, then said, 'Derek Johnson would like you to call him back at your leisure. No rush I believe were his exact words.'

No rush. No rush? From the kid who always sounded as if

he lived on a pure raspberry cordial diet? 'Do you have any idea who that was?' he asked.

'Sure I do,' she said, standing and tugging her floral blouse back into place as she came around the desk. She flapped the note at him. 'It was the boy who's going to be the number one draft pick. But he's also a boy whose mother never set nearly enough boundaries when he was a kid. He called me *love. Love!* Little stirrer. If Beau even talked to anyone like that…'

She didn't get the chance to say what she would do, as by that stage Danny had already lost it. He laughed out loud. So loud Brooke stopped talking and just stared at him. She frowned, a small vertical crinkle appearing between her brows. 'What's so funny?'

'You,' he said, taking the chance to drink in her face, her earnest, expressive, lovely face.

She took a deep breath, then said, 'I'm sorry. I should have left well enough alone. But a ringing phone to me is like a dripping tap, or crumbs on the kitchen bench. Nobody else is going to look after it, so it becomes a compulsion to do what I have to do. Sorry.'

'Sorry?' he repeated. 'Brooke, you were perfect.'

She blinked up at him as though nobody had ever called her perfect before. And this was a woman who deserved to be called that and more. Who deserved to be built up and praised and glorified and adored.

Before he knew what he was about to do, his hands cupped her cheeks and he leaned in and kissed her. Hard. Fast. A kiss born of thanks. And joy. And relief that she had actually known who the caller was, when Lucille wouldn't have had a clue, and also that she had somehow managed to schmooze fiery Derek Johnson with nothing more than her charm and her dulcet tones.

When he pulled away, only then did he realise what he'd

done. He'd kissed her. His mouth had met hers. He could feel the imprint of her soft lips branded against his own. The sense memory so strong if he closed his eyes he could imagine he was kissing her still.

He wished he were kissing her still. Again. More. And this time he'd make it count, not let it pass him by before he'd even allowed the whole momentous moment to wash over him. His hands remained where they were. Framing her face. Revelling in the feel of her soft skin beneath his palms.

She looked up at him, her eyes glistening, shocked and wide as he had ever seen them. And then her tongue darted out and licked her bottom lip before her teeth followed, drawing its fullness into her mouth.

Danny could barely suppress his ensuing groan. He let his hands drop, but she didn't step away.

She could have. For sure. She could have taken a couple of steps backwards, as good as creating a gulf between them, giving him the sign that there would be no more kissing today. If ever.

But she did not. She just stood there, close enough to touch, close enough that he could smell her sweet apple scent, close enough that he could make out the dozen different shades of green in her beautiful big eyes staring up at him as if she'd never seen him before.

Not knowing what else to do, he reached out and plucked the note from her hand. She gave no resistance. If he was in the mood for being fanciful he could have imagined that was because she was as shaken as he was. Her muscles struggling to remember how to work. Her senses numb to all but the tingling sensation in her lips.

'Do you mind if I call him back now?' he asked, his voice hoarse.

She shook her head.

'I'll take it in my office. Do you want to come with me? Or do you want to wait here for Lucille?'

She shook her head again. She was shell-shocked. Not angry. Not uncomfortable. But stunned into silence. After one small peck.

He wondered what she would look like if he kissed her properly. If he took his time. Took a long slow moment to lean in, sharing breaths and anticipation for almost too long before their lips touched. If he pressed, and pulled away. If he traced her lower lip with the tip of his tongue. If he coaxed her mouth apart, and tilted his head just so...

And right then Lucille reappeared. 'Hey, boss! Buckley and I have been having a catch-up. He's in your office now.'

She looked up and saw Brooke, standing still as a statue. And then back at him. He only hoped she couldn't read his recent imaginings in his face. She placed a half-drunk cup of herbal tea on her desk and knelt one leg on her chair as her bright eyes kept shifting from one of them to the other. 'So what did I miss?'

'An important phone call,' Danny grumbled. 'From Derek Johnson.'

Lucille blinked up at him and shrugged. She had no idea who the kid was. Yet Brooke had. Brooke, who knew how to schmooze on the phone like no one he'd ever seen. Brooke, who had lived and breathed a sporting life for eight years. Brooke, who was looking for a job. Brooke, who he adored from the tip of her blonde head to her currently scrunching toes.

He hadn't been kidding when he'd told her she would be an asset to his business. Back then he'd been primarily thinking with something other than his head. Though that something had still been right. She'd be an asset. But she'd also be a distraction. Was he strong enough to harness one and ignore the other? Would he be able to fight the urge to kiss her every time she made a successful phone call?

Somehow he doubted it. His restraint was getting weaker every day. And all the while his attraction to her was growing, blossoming into other areas. Inescapable areas such as tenderness for her kids. Concerns over whether she could ever be happy working in some dead-end job just to keep her kids in clothes. Into strong, emotion-deep, impetuous feelings that were so tangled inside him it would take more strength than even he had to unravel them.

'Can you get Brooke a coffee, Lucille? Then set her up in Johnno's office and get her online. Johnno's in Boston,' he told Brooke. 'We're about to get a Tasmanian kid signed up to the Red Sox.'

'Bailey Montgomery,' she said, the first words out of her mouth since their kiss.

He smiled. *Welcome back.* 'That's right. It's nice to know there are women in my life who realise the sports news is more than just the chance to make a cup of tea.'

Lucille merely grinned at him way too knowingly. His smile faded in an instant and he fought back the urge to hiss at her.

'Go with Lucille,' he said to Brooke. 'She'll set you up, and I'll come check on you in a bit, okay?'

Brooke squared her shoulders, obviously preparing herself for the job hunt ahead, though from the look on her face he could have thought she was going to a torture chamber. He actually felt her distress as if it was happening to him.

'Are you sure you're ready for this?' he asked.

'I'll be fine,' she said. 'You just do what you have to do. Pretend I'm not here.'

'Oh, honey,' Lucille said, rolling her eyes and bustling around the desk to take Brooke by the elbow, 'if you think for a second he can pretend you're not here then I would hazard a guess I'm the only woman in Danny's life who knows there's *more* to life than the sports news.'

Danny took that as his cue to leave. 'My office door will be open. Don't hesitate to come in any time, okay?'

Brooke's expression was caught between wanting him to save her from Lucille's clutches and half hoping he hadn't understood Lucille's cryptic words as clearly as she had.

But he more than understood. He adored her. He wanted her. And now that he'd had a taste of those soft lips, he knew there was no turning back. Lucille knew it. Emily knew it. Hell, he was pretty sure even Simone knew it. He wondered how long he had before Brooke realised it too.

He gave her one last half smile, then walked down the hall and into his office. He sat behind his desk and ran a hand over his chin, not even nearly ready to tackle the likes of Derek Johnson.

For he knew it would take more than Brooke's squared shoulders for him to forget she was sitting two small rooms away. It would take more than a hurricane. An earthquake. Or a thousand first round draft picks awaiting his call.

CHAPTER NINE

AFTER dinner that night Brooke called Simone's mobile. Lily told her all about the shells they had collected on the beach that day, and Beau gave her a complete minute by minute rundown of his first day at his new school.

She realised halfway through that her hand was clutched to her heart. She knew that these nights away were good for them. That it was healthy for them to spend time with people other than her. And they were good for Simone too, gave her people to focus on other than herself. But it still didn't stop the empty ache in her heart, knowing that she wouldn't be kissing them goodnight that evening.

Simone came on quickly at the end. 'All done?'

'Yes,' she said on a sigh. 'Give them both an extra kiss from me.'

'Shall do. Now, don't do anything I wouldn't do,' Simone said, 'unless, of course, Danny is involved, then I give you permission to go for your life.'

And then she hung up, leaving Brooke staring at the phone as though it had emitted a rude sound.

'So do you want to watch a DVD or something?' the man himself asked.

'Why not?' She followed Danny into his warm, welcoming den and slumped into a soft couch while he flicked through his DVD library. It would be a good idea to drown out her thoughts with 5.1 surround sound. 'So long as it has adult themes and there is no mention of Harry Potter, I'll be a happy woman.'

'What's your preference?' he asked, flicking a dark glance over his shoulder.

'Just like Beau, I love cops and shooting and stuff, but unlike him I have nobody telling me what I can and can't watch.'

Danny smiled; she could feel it caressing her in the semi-darkness. She waited for her nerves to itch from being alone with him for real for the first time, well, ever, without Cal or the kids or his staff acting as chaperons. But they didn't make a peep. Perhaps she was simply too tired to feel anything much after the day she'd had. Or maybe a good week of holding herself in check had begun to pay off and whatever silly kind of crush she had been indulging in had dissolved away.

'So did you find a winner today?' he asked.

She sighed and leant back into the seat, tucking her legs beneath her. 'If I was a third year apprentice hairdresser, a university graduate or a research scientist then I would have had my pick.'

'But, since you are none of those things...'

'It turns out I am *not* a lot of things. I'm not experienced enough to work in an office. Available enough to work in retail. Or young enough to take part in an experimental pro-gramme at the university, which is the greatest pity as it was paying the best money.' She lowered her face into her hands. 'It's official. Somewhere along the way, I have lost my mojo.'

'Your mojo?' he repeated.

'You know, when you're young and the world's your oyster

and you have this magic and hope and innate cool that seems to set you apart?'

'I know what mojo is,' he said. 'I just wasn't aware you thought yours was missing.'

'Mine isn't missing, it simply is no more. The determination that got me to England when I was eighteen and straight into a job at London's coolest club has vanished. I certainly wasn't the prettiest there. I didn't have the biggest boobs, or the longest legs, or the loudest laugh. But I had some kind of mojo. Bankers, lawyers, hot-shot TV execs—they were once lining up for my phone number.'

'And Cal,' he said, as if she could have forgotten.

'And Cal,' she repeated, noticing he'd been the one to bring him up again. She looked up at him through the gaps between her fingers to find he was frowning at the back of a DVD case. 'But along the way, in amongst raising two rowdy kids, and expending every other bit of energy trying to keep Cal's life organised while he lived most of it thousands of miles away, my mojo has gone belly-up. Not one of the people I phoned today even wanted to meet me. I tell you, it's depressing.'

'They're idiots,' he said.

'That's what I think! But maybe I need to get that in writing. You could pretend I had worked for you before and be my reference.'

'Why pretend?'

She lowered her hands. 'I thought you'd given up on that idea by now. And remember,' she said, jabbing at her chest, 'inexperienced, not all that available and no longer eighteen.'

Danny put the DVD into the machine. 'I still need a PA. You have a killer instinct on the phone which I witnessed first hand today. You know the business. And simply having you around might scare Lucille into picking up her act.'

He stood, his large form blocking out the light from the one golden lamp sending its smooth rays into a pool of light below the screen. Suddenly he was dark, mysterious Danny again, all broad shoulders and lean hips encased in black. And, just like that, her nerves came back with a vengeance. Her nerves, a terrifying tumbling mixture of feelings and the dull ache of desire. Damn it! If only she'd had her mojo intact she might have been able to combat such feelings. But without it she was completely unprotected.

'What about Lily?' she asked, staring up at him still.

'The spare office across from mine is big enough for a desk and a play area for Lily. Or there are at least three day care facilities within a stone's throw of the office. Lots of young families in St Kilda nowadays.'

Brooke breathed in deep. Boy, was he tempting?

It. It was tempting. Dealing with that punk kid on the phone today had felt satisfying. As did the thought of working in an industry she knew, in which people knew of her. It would be her chance to show them all that the woman behind the man was more than just that. Always had been, always would be. If her mojo needed any kind of kick-start to come back out of hiding, she was pretty certain that was it.

'That's a really tempting offer, Danny. But you have given so much of yourself for the sake of my family already.'

The opening credits of the movie started to play, but she didn't even notice it bar a bright blue light travelling down Danny's right side, showcasing strong forearms at the base of the rolled-up sleeves of his black shirt. His collar was undone, revealing a manly throat and a light spray of dark hair on his chest.

He moved away from the screen and sat on the couch next to her. He leant back against the armrest so that he was facing her and not the screen, which had begun to play a Sting song over the top of the image of licking flames. She knew the movie but couldn't place it. Couldn't place much with Danny's right knee resting mere centimetres from the bottom of her bare right foot.

'I haven't done it for your family, Brooke,' he said, his voice low.

'Oh,' she said. She felt her cheeks turn pink. 'For Cal. Sorry, you know I meant for Cal.'

Perhaps it was just the heady combination of tangy citrus scent and male attention that was making her feel this way whenever he was near. The skin tingles, the jitters, the nervous knots in her stomach. Her hormones were on red alert since they'd had no release in so very long. And Danny just happened to be in the way.

He shook his head. 'I haven't done it for Cal either.'

'Oh.' Yes, *oh* again. *Oh* was a fine small word, for it summed up exactly how she felt. Small and out of her depth. Especially in view of those acute golden eyes, now lit by the warmth of the lamp.

Who was she kidding? The nervous knots didn't happen around every nice-looking, nice-smelling guy she'd run into over the past months. Heck, Mel Gibson was now parading around on the wall in front of her and she didn't give a hoot. It only ever happened around Danny.

Danny, who earlier that day had taken her face in his large hands and kissed her. A short, sweet kiss born of thanks and relief and good humour. Not love, or care, or uncontrollable lust by any means, but in that moment her libido hadn't cared one lick. For it had been a kiss that had curled her toes and uncurled all sorts of feelings she thought had turned to dust long ago. And those feelings were now in full control.

'So who have you done it all for?' she asked, her voice far stronger than she felt.

He breathed out, sharp and fast, as though coming to some long-fought conclusion. 'Brooke, come on.'

'Come on what?'

'Don't make me say it.'

She slowly unhooked her feet from under her and ended up leaning on her left hip, supporting her weight on her left hand, leaning in towards him. 'I'm going to need you to say it.'

His brow tightened. His cheeks hollowed. His eyes narrowed. And then he shifted, barely, but enough that he suddenly felt closer. Close enough that she felt she was breathing in the very air that he breathed out.

'I invited you here to stay with me,' he said, his voice a sexy rumble in the near darkness, 'not for the sake of your family, or out of some sense of loyalty to Cal. I did it only for you.'

She knew it. Had always known it. Long before Simone had even suggested it. She had resisted it, had put up walls and created blocking mechanisms, and for the most part ignored it. But she knew it.

He was feeling as torn as she was; she could see it in his dark clouded eyes, in the tension in his arms. But now, truly alone with him for the first time ever, as a single woman in desperate need of a little bit of magic in her life, all that need was just too much for this one female to resist.

With a whispered sigh that spoke of *what the hell?* with a good dash of *what the hell am I getting myself into?* Brooke leaned in the rest of the way and kissed him.

For a brief second as his lips lay still beneath her own she wondered if she had made a colossal error of judgement. But within another second Danny was involved without a doubt.

His strong muscular arms swept around her, hugging her so tight he all but lifted her into his lap.

And his kiss, oh, his kiss…

Brooke thought all she was looking for was to release the pressure of the mounting tension between them, but his kiss showed her how wrong she had been.

As he drew her ever closer, kissed her ever deeper, her knees trembled, her skin zinged and every other part of her ached for more. His kiss felt as if it had been a long time coming, as if every part of her life, good and bad, had been leading to this one moment.

His hand tucked beneath the rise of her T-shirt, scorching the skin of her lower back with his gentle touch, his little finger hooking into the band of her jeans.

She wrapped her arms around his neck. His skin, warmed by a smouldering inner fire, was so hot against her cool fingers. He just made her feel so small. Delicate. Feminine. Danny's aura was just so vast, so all-encompassing and so utterly male.

She knew all she had to do was let go and this would only get better. To stop thinking and be caught up in every tiny little new experience and just let it happen, wash over her, numb her to everything else that had gone wrong in her life until she was nothing but a mass of warmth and feeling and exquisiteness in his strong arms.

She moved, sliding herself along the couch until she was on her knees straddling him. A hot shiver rocked through Danny's body and he let his hands drop away to softly cradle her backside.

Suddenly feeling in utter control, for the first time in as long as she could remember, Brooke let her hands slide from behind Danny's neck so that she could cup his face. She slowed the kiss. On purpose. Her insides threatened to melt as she simply allowed herself to experience every lick of pleasure.

After what seemed like hours, he shifted his head back. A groan escaped her lips.

'Don't you dare stop,' she whispered.

'I need to take a breath,' he said against her mouth.

She smiled. A smile full of confidence and conquest. The feeling infusing her with pure gratification. And then she ignored his request and kissed him again, this time slowly, sparingly—just. She had never felt sexier in her entire life.

For she knew that this was a guy who worshipped her. She *knew* it. Like a blinding flash of light, she knew it. Why she hadn't been able to see it all before, she had no idea. But now he lay back and simply took her ministrations as if he was a man close to death in a desert and she was his last sip of water.

'You're just too bloody good at this,' he whispered.

She lifted her head long enough to answer, 'Surprising, considering it has been so long between drinks.'

And then he flinched. His strong thighs growing tight beneath hers.

'What's wrong?' she asked, her voice husky and soft.

He pulled away further, until he was out of reach. Not physically. If she wanted to, she could have leaned down and continued. But emotionally he was gone from her. Cool, distant, aloof, just as she had always imagined him to be.

Her face burned hot and she wanted to slap herself silly for opening her big mouth and saying whatever it was that had taken those beautiful lips from her. Those beautiful feelings of control. But she couldn't even remember a word she'd said. All she could remember was those lips.

'What's wrong?' she asked again.

He shook his head; his eyes were dark and clouded. She wanted to grab him by the lapels and shake him until he unclouded them. Until he opened up to her with the same sweetness and openness she had felt in that one kiss. The same honesty and promise.

But then he lifted a hand and ran it across his mouth. Wiping away her kiss? And Brooke felt the painful wash of embarrassment slap against her cheeks until they burned.

She lifted herself off him, hunkered back into the other corner of the couch and threw her arms in the air. 'Well, now I'm totally confused!'

Danny glanced across at her, his eyes still unreadable. 'Why did you kiss me, Brooke?'

She shook her head. Her blood boiled with remaining heat from their kiss and with the added scorch of embarrassment and confusion. Her skin ached from no longer having his touch. But she kept her distance all the same. She stared at the screen.

'Why did you kiss me, Brooke?' he asked again. 'This time I need you to say it.'

She let out a long slow breath. 'I thought this was what you wanted. Simone told me so for so many years I had begun to believe it!'

'You kissed me because Simone told you you should,' he said, his voice so cool and calm, so lacking in passion, she wanted to scream.

'Yeah,' she scoffed, 'that's it. I'm famous for doing as my sister tells me to. That's why I spent my inheritance in three months flat when I moved to London alone. That's why I married a guy I barely knew when Simone's first words when she heard my plans were that I would regret it. And *that's* why I kissed you just now.'

She turned to him, her eyes wide with anger. At herself and at him for not coming clean either. He had been as into the kiss as she was. If this was what he wanted, if *she* was what he wanted, then why the hell wasn't he leaping in feet first?

'You so pride yourself on being honest, Danny. But you invited me here. You have spent the past week looking longingly my way and inventing girlfriends and spending as much time with me as you could possibly spare. So be honest with me now. What do you want from me?'

'Not this,' he said.

Her breaths grew strong and laboured as her utter confusion rose. 'Not what exactly?'

He turned to fully face her and she saw that he wasn't as cool as he seemed. His hair was a spiky mess from where her frantic fingers had taken hold, his eyes were shining and fierce, his shirt was half-untucked and his chest rose and fell as if he could scarcely draw breath.

He was so sexy her heart thundered in her chest and her breasts felt instantly heavy. If she wasn't so emotionally bruised she would have been back in his lap in half a second.

'I don't want you like this, Brooke,' he said, his voice conversely calm. 'Not as some sort of revenge, or self-punishment, or as a way to clear your head, or feel good about yourself, or not to have to think about how alone you'll be tonight without your kids.'

'That's not what I was doing—'

'Brooke,' he said, the tone of his voice cutting through her excuses like a hot knife through butter, 'I know you too well.'

She flopped her head against the back of the couch and closed her eyes. Exhausted. Mentally and emotionally. Wishing she could wipe away the memory of that kiss as easily as Danny had wiped his mouth. But she couldn't. She knew that she would remember every single sensation of that kiss for the rest of her life.

Danny slowly shifted, his weight making the fabric beneath Brooke's backside shift and roll. He wanted so badly to reach out and place a hand on the back of her head, his warm fingers tucking beneath strands of her hair. To coax her until she sighed with pleasure. And then he wanted to kiss her again. More. Forever.

Her eyes remained closed. She breathed in hard, her chest rising and falling, her exposed throat lit by a shaft of light from the nearby lamp. His dream girl was right now on his couch, vulnerable, open to him. And she had kissed him. *She* had kissed *him*.

Before this it had seemed a beautiful pipedream. If he was in the mood for being cynical, he might have thought his feelings for her, and the fact that she was so completely out of bounds, had been a terribly handy excuse for not connecting fully with anyone else. For keeping his life his own and for not falling into the same trap his mother had time and again. Maybe once… But not now. Not any more.

Now their attraction was out in the open. Now there was nothing between them bar two feet of sofa and his fractured self-control. And it terrified him. For she hadn't in any way intimated she had kissed him for the same reasons he'd kissed her. He was no closer to knowing how she felt about him than he had been an hour earlier.

He realised then that she was looking at him. Her head had tilted and she was watching him. Her wide green eyes filled with concern. She uncurled her left hand and reached out to cover his, which rested flat on his thigh, and said, 'Danny, I—'

'Shush,' he said, cutting her off. 'It's okay.'

'No, it's not. I don't…I can't lose you,' she said, her voice thin and shaky. 'I can't lose your friendship. Not over something so crazy as a kiss.'

'You won't lose me, Brooke,' he said, 'not ever. I promise.'

But, even as he said the words, they sat heavy upon his

chest. She would never lose him, but there was a very real possibility that he might yet lose her. If he made the wrong move, if he pushed too hard.

But, then again, could he truly put everything—his loyalty to Cal, his very real fear of commitment, the reputation of his business—on the line for her if she wasn't willing to take as big a risk for him? The struggle almost tore him in half, for as she watched him, as her swollen lips enticed him and her warm, willing body tempted him, every rebellious inch of him simply wanted to take whatever she was willing to give.

She gave him a watery smile. 'I don't know why you stick by me, Danny. I've been a great fool many times over. I make terrible decisions and then live by them as though they are written in stone. I'm not terribly tidy. I can't cook. I have a short temper. I'm the walking wounded from my last relationship. The closest I ever come to playing any sport is yoga or chasey. I must surely be the bane of your existence.'

'You really want to know why I stick by you, Brooke?' he asked. He probably should never have offered such an insight. And she should probably have said no and left it at that. Her confidence was shot. Her trust abused. Her every relationship demanding. In the past few months she'd lost her husband— a man who had extinguished her capacity to believe in herself. She had lost her home, her lifestyle and any friends she'd thought she had. She was holding on to control of her life with her fingernails. The last thing Danny wanted to be was one more complication in her life. But when she merely looked deep into his eyes and said nothing he couldn't help himself.

So, with a sigh of resignation, he turned to her, his eyes roving over every inch of her face, and said, 'You are kind. You are ferociously protective of those you love. You are as spirited as you are tender. You are as funny as you are surprising. And a man would have to be blind not to find himself drowning in those great green eyes of yours.'

For several moments Brooke just stared at him. Danny felt as though his senses had suddenly gone into overload. The movie played softly in the background. The ribbed fabric of the sofa bit gently into the backs of his forearms. He could even sense the movement and tension of the neck muscles keeping his head upright.

When she finally found her voice again, she said, 'My eyes aren't green, they're hazel.'

His focus shifted until he looked deep into each eye, one at a time. Then he ignored all good judgement and gave into pure need and reached up and laid a warm hand upon her cheek, running his thumb across her cheek bone. Back and forth.

'Nah,' he drawled, his face creasing into the beginnings of the first smile he'd managed to summon since she'd kissed it away. 'They are every shade of green. Vibrant, dark, shadowed and bright. The colour of new leaves and old forests. And altogether the loveliest green eyes this soul has ever seen.'

She reached up and placed a hand over his, pausing a moment before she curled her fingers around his and pulled his hand away from her face.

He swore he saw tears in her eyes then. Great shimmering waves of tears threatening to pour from her big beautiful eyes. He knew if that happened he'd be undone. He'd throw himself on her mercy. And she'd never respect him and he wouldn't blame her.

He uncurled his fingers from hers and laid her hand on her lap and then pulled himself from the sofa. 'I think it best we call it a night. Unless you want to watch the rest of the movie.'

Her cheek creased into a half smile. 'What would be the point? I didn't see any of the first half, either.'

Danny shoved his hands into his trouser pockets to stop himself from reaching down and hauling her into his arms and kissing her until her limbs went lax with pleasure and that sexy half smile was far too tired to come out to tempt him any more.

'Be ready by eight. You start work at my office tomorrow, okay?'

'Thank you,' she said.

Brooke watched Danny walk away.

She took a shaky breath. Her emotions were quite simply ragged. She had absolutely no idea what had just happened. But one thing she did know was that everything had changed.

She was no longer the woman she had been three months before. She was no longer the bedraggled, disappointed casualty of a disastrous marriage. But neither was she entirely sure that she was the voluptuous, panting, yearning woman who had made a move on Danny just now.

Nevertheless she *had* kissed him. And he'd kissed her back. Things were never going to be the same again. No matter how many jokes she made and how sweet he was to her afterwards. They'd stepped over an invisible line tonight and there was no going back.

She ran her hands hard and fast over her face, trying to wipe away the thrumming feeling still scooting through her veins even though he was no longer in the room. Though she knew the only way to negate all of that energy would be to follow that gorgeous view all the way to his bedroom. To see if the promise in his eyes, and in his touch, could really truly be kept. Damn the consequences.

But she wouldn't. She couldn't.

Because she knew that if *this* man didn't keep his promises to her, those wounds she carried with her every day would never be healed.

CHAPTER TEN

AT FIVE minutes past nine the next morning Brooke introduced her backside to her new office chair in her very own office at the Good Sports Agency. The room was huge, the desk massive, the bookshelves filled with almanacs and photo albums and DVDs of football matches. It had a wide-screen laptop and a phone with so many switches and buttons it would have looked more at home on the console of a spaceship.

She imagined how the desk would look with photos of the kids. It would look fantastic, she thought. She leant back and put her feet up on the desk for just a moment, allowing herself to feel relieved that nothing had happened between them the night before and this situation might actually work itself out.

Danny never needed to know that twelve hours later she still felt the imprint of his lips, the tender stroke of his hand on her arm and the sweetness of his words. That could be her little secret. And she was very very good at keeping secrets.

The phone rang at reception and she slid her feet back to the floor and sat on her hands. Beyond that was the murmur of another dozen voices. The soft jangle of computer keys. The overlapping of TV noise in every office. It lent a real energy to the place. An energy that infused her. Making her right leg jiggle.

Or maybe that was just the fact that every time she heard footsteps she thought it might be Danny.

The car drive into St Kilda had been tense. They'd made small talk, discussed dinner plans and grocery lists. She'd filled him in on her need to leave early to pick up Lily from Simone's and then Beau from school. He'd insisted it would work out fine if they took the one car. Until they'd bumped hands reaching for the stereo volume then jumped apart as though burned, and not said another word to one another until they'd reached the office.

Overnight their relationship had become about small talk and avoiding sex. Heck, they were acting like a regular old married couple. She only hoped they'd get over it and fast and go back to being…what? Friends? Somehow that word didn't even hope to encapsulate what Danny Finch meant to her.

Her phone buzzed. She slowly picked up the handset and held it to her ear.

'Hey, Brooke,' Lucille said.

'Hey, Lucille.'

'Did you figure out the percolator?'

'Yes, thanks.'

'Excellent. Then you're ready. Line one's for Danny. Good luck!'

Lucille hung up, leaving Brooke with nothing but empty air. She hung up too, rolled her shoulders, shook out her hair, then picked up the phone and pressed the flashing red light.

'Danny Finch's office,' she said. 'This is Brooke.'

There was a pause on the end of the phone. It could have been because the caller was expecting Danny himself. But it felt…different. It made the hairs on the back of her neck stand on end. Maybe it was one of those salespeople trying to get her to change her long distance phone plans; they always seemed to pause before talking.

She considered simply hanging up when a female voice said, 'Brooke Findlay.'

'It is,' she said, her fine neck hairs now standing so stiff they were all but saluting.

'This is Rachel Cross from *Sports Scene*. We spoke on the phone at Danny's house several days ago about a possible interview. Are…are you *working* for Danny now?'

She just couldn't win! The fates could have given her a screaming footballer, a whinging cyclist or a desperate swimmer to placate. But no, instead she had a member of the press with a fresh lead on a story that, according to the paper inches still dedicated to it, everyone in town was still excited over.

Brooke bit at the inside of her lip to stop herself from telling the woman that she was in fact Danny's transvestite alter ego. That surely would have stopped any other rumours. But somehow she didn't think Danny would appreciate the joke as much as she would.

'What can I do for you, Ms Cross?' she asked instead.

'You did ask me to call Danny back at the office last week, and so here I am. Calling.'

'Right, well, I'm sorry but he's in a meeting right now. I can certainly take a message. Hang on while I find a pen.'

She opened the top desk drawer and instead found a small gift-wrapped box. She stared at it for a few long moments. The card sticking out the top had her name on it.

She glanced out the windows into the hallway but there was nobody there. She looked back to the drawer, pulled out the package with as much care as if it had been a ticking bomb. She opened the card. It read:

Didn't you know that every girl gets a special present on her first day at work? It's one of the million cool things about starting a new job.

Danny

She laughed, then covered her mouth to stop herself from sobbing. The guy had used almost the exact words he'd used to make Beau feel better on his first day of school. Danny was something special. So utterly special.

A knock came at the door.

Brooke flinched, and looked up to find Emily smiling at her from the doorway and looking gorgeous in a vanilla-coloured trouser suit. Excellent. What had she done to anger the gods today? Seriously?

She held up a finger, and when she saw that it was shaking she brought her hand quickly back to clutch at the edge of the desk.

'Brooke?' the phone said.

'What, yes? Oh, sorry.' She shoved the package aside and found a pen and a pad of notepaper. 'You were saying.'

'I would love to have you in next Thursday if you are free. If you have ever seen our show, you will know that Martin is in no way sensationalistic. He is a down-to-earth, dedicated journalist who just wants to tell the true stories behind the glitz and glamour of the professional sports scene. We know your story would touch a lot of hearts.'

'You mean you want Danny,' Brooke said when she had finished taking notes.

'Well, as I said before, if you would prefer for him to come along as well then that would be great,' Rachel said slowly, as though talking to someone not quite all there, 'but you're the one the country wants to hear from. And I can promise you, once the punters all get to see that you're okay, there will be closure.'

Closure? The word made itself at home in Brooke's sub-conscious. It was a seriously comforting word. Like a freshly scrubbed blackboard. But any such closure was not something she wished to sell for public consumption.

'Ms Cross, I don't see how a television interview in which I spill my private thoughts to the country will give me any sense of closure.'

'Perhaps not. But it will give it to the country.'

The country. The ones who bought the magazines that fuelled the high payments to paparazzi who hid in bushes to get photos of her kids. As far as she was concerned, the country could go jump. She slowly let her pen fall to the desk. 'So you have no message for Danny, then.'

'Well, only so far as you want to tell him what we've talked about today.'

'I guess we're done, then.'

'Until next time,' Rachel said.

'Goodbye,' Brooke said, and then she hung up the phone. She looked up and saw Emily was still in her doorway. 'Hi,' she said, shooting to her feet. 'Sorry. Come in, come in.'

'So you're really working here?' Emily said as she eased into the room with all the grace of a dancer and slid her elegant form into a chair, crossing her feet at the ankles.

Brooke straightened her pastel-pink blouse and tugged at her denim skirt, then gave up. There was no way she could ever compare to this woman in the glamour stakes. Too many years of being covered from head to toe in baby biscuit had simply knocked that out of her. 'I am,' she said, 'for the moment.'

Emily raised an eyebrow and left a gap for Brooke to fill her in.

'I'm not sure how much Danny has told you about my situation.'

Emily smiled, and Brooke knew it was probably a great deal. But she didn't really mind. She liked Emily. She seemed straight down the line. What you saw was what you got. And what Brooke saw was actually pretty great. Maybe she should encourage Danny to try again with her. Or maybe she could just stop thinking about him period. Or maybe she could just flap her wings and fly away.

'I need a job, and he needs someone between him and Lucille or the two of them will kill one another for sure.'

Emily laughed. 'Oh, don't sell yourself short. Just now Danny told me how you handled Derek Johnson on the phone the other day. It seems that behind that yummy-mummy exterior you have a dark side. I thought I liked you, and now I know I do.'

Brooke couldn't help but smile back. 'Thanks. I think.'

'Mmm,' Emily said. 'So what's with the gift?'

Brooke followed her line of sight to see the small square box. 'I haven't had the chance to open it yet.'

'Don't let me stop you.' She leaned forward, resting her fine chin on a closed fist.

Brooke tried to think of a reason why not to—religious, cultural, even something to do with the alignment of her stars, but she came up with nothing. So she pulled on the white ribbon, sliding it from around the beautiful green box. Green, not hazel, she thought, and her skin began to tingle as though Danny was standing behind her.

She took a deep breath and opened the clasp to find a beautiful silver necklace with a locket. With shaking hands, she lifted it out of its case and opened the locket to find two pictures of her kids. Smiling at the camera. At her. With such love she couldn't see through the sheen in her eyes.

'May I?' Emily said, holding out a hand.

Brooke handed over the gift. Emily spent a few moments admiring it before she said, 'We're not actually dating, you know.'

Brooke let out a breath she didn't even know she'd been holding, then cleared her throat and looked up at her guest. Emily was now watching her. Carefully, but with no malice. No disappointment. No resentment. Not a lick.

'I know,' Brooke admitted, though she'd had no idea how relieved she would be to hear it from this woman's mouth.

Emily handed the necklace back to Brooke. 'We tried a couple of years back, but it never quite stuck. Which is a great pity as he has the greatest butt on any man I have ever met. And I work with footballers day in and day out.'

Brooke laughed, as she was meant to do, but she left the statement well enough alone. She was fixated on the guy's eyes, his hands, his lips, his voice—she didn't need another part of him to add to the list of things she wanted more of. 'There's always a chance you could try again.'

Emily raised one thin eyebrow. 'What would be the point? Especially when I've known for ages that he's madly in love with someone else.'

Thankfully, Brooke's phone began to buzz.

'Anyhow, I must run,' Emily said. 'Football players to hire and fire.' She headed for the door, but turned at the last second and wrapped long slim fingers around the doorframe. 'One piece of advice.'

Brooke let the phone keep ringing and gave a small nod.

'To quote a clever sportswear company who know what they are talking about—*Just do it*. And to quote myself, a woman who has been around the traps—there is no harsher mistress than regret.'

Brooke suddenly itched to confess everything to this woman. To tell her about the kiss, the aftermath and how the two of them had gone on pretending things were as they had always been. To tell her about her sleepless night, and her swaying between wanting Danny and not wanting to deal with the consequences of wanting him. And with not really being any more sure of his feelings for her than she had been before the kiss. But her built-in reticence came to the fore and she kept her mouth shut.

And then Emily was gone, leaving Brooke with the locket clasped tight within her sweating palm, and three phone lines on her console lit up as if her spaceship was going down.

Brooke drove around to the St Kilda hotel to pick up Lily during her lunch break. She hadn't been able to find Danny, but she also hadn't really looked for him. At that point she didn't quite know what on earth to say to him if she did.

Simone answered the boutique hotel room door in her suit, putting an earring in her right ear. No hugs, no kisses, no sisterly smiles. Just a nod and then, 'Excellent. Right on time. I've checked out already as I have to go into work this afternoon.'

'You should have called,' Brooke said, wringing her hands. 'I could have come earlier.'

'No, no,' Simone said, still trying to find the earring hole in her right ear. 'I wouldn't have wanted to get you in trouble with the boss.'

'Where's Lily?'

'Down at the pool with Jerry. He wanted to say hello before the kids left. She's saying goodbye to her imaginary pet turtle, Mickey. Mickey stays with us every time we come here, but never wants to go home with her. Funny kid.'

'It's a comfort thing,' Brooke said absently. 'Like the

feather boa. Like Beau's pillow.' *Like me and Danny? Is that all it is? Is that why I'm hanging on so tight? Why I kissed him, but couldn't tell him that the decision to kiss him had been all mine?*

Brooke sat on the edge of the bed. Then, feeling too full of nervous energy, stood again and moved over to the window, looking down at the gorgeous beach view.

'Don't panic,' Simone said on a laugh. 'She won't take long. You can get back to your man ASAP.'

Brooke turned from the window and suddenly couldn't hold it in any more. 'I kissed him.'

'The imaginary turtle?' Simone asked.

'No, you ninny. Danny.'

Simone's dark hazel eyes so similar to her own opened up wide and her mouth hung open. She was truly shocked. Brooke wasn't sure she had ever seen Simone truly shocked. She usually hid all that kind of stuff so well behind sarcasm and apathy.

'Well, there you go,' Simone said, sitting on the edge of the bed, her earring forgotten. 'I mean, it's been coming forever but I truly never thought I'd see the day.'

Brooke sat next to her big sister, facing the far wall with its incongruous print of an English country garden. 'Well, it happened. I kissed him. And it was…amazing. It was like fireworks and shooting stars and like I'd never done it before, but like we'd done it so many times we'd become the world's best. Then he told me that he wanted to drown in my eyes and then he went to bed. Alone. And then today, he bought me this.' She opened the top two buttons of her high-necked blouse and closed her eyes tight as she showed off the locket.

'That bastard,' Simone said, with feeling.

Brooke opened one eye.

'Well, the guy is obviously no good,' Simone said. 'Looking after you for all these years, giving up his home to you in your hour of need, buying you gifts and opening up to you like that. It's all a cover, surely. Nobody can be that perfect. Does he have a wife locked in the attic *à la Jane Eyre?*'

With each sardonic word Brooke felt more and more short of breath. She was the one who was drowning here. 'Do you always have to do that?'

'What did I do?'

'Can't you give me one lick of sympathy? Or empathy. Or even just pretend to care that I am in a state about this? Just for once in your life?'

Simone's mouth clamped shut and her cheeks turned pink. It was a look that meant Brooke would receive the silent treatment for a fortnight, and then everything would go back to normal. It was their way. One she was sick to death of.

She didn't have any really close female friends. The ones she'd thought she'd had had disappeared in a plume of exhaust the moment Cal had died. She had a couple of new ones that she was looking forward to cultivating. But for the moment the only person she could count on to take some of the heat was her own flesh and blood.

So, before she could swallow the words, Brooke blurted out, 'Can't you see I need your help?'

Simone stilled. And Brooke faltered. 'I mean I thought you were offering that night, and I don't want to impose and...'

Simone held up a hand, cutting her off. 'Stop. Rewind. Go back to the part where you need my help.'

Brooke took a deep breath and dived in. 'Everything is so muddled in my head. My anger towards Cal. My sadness that he is really gone for good. And Danny is in the middle of all that. He was Cal's confidant, and his contemporary, a guy who lived the same life for a number of years when he was playing representative cricket. And then again he's been *my* stalwart, a constant in *my* life for so many years. And now that I had to go and kiss him, everything has changed, whether I want it to or not. We can't go back, but I'm not sure how to go forward or if it is even the best thing for me right now to do so.'

Brooke took a breath and turned to her sister. 'The ability to look after myself is so important to me, asking for help, from *anybody,* for me is akin to chewing off my own foot. A last resort. But I'm asking you now. Can you help me?'

Simone bit at the inside of her lip, a move Brooke knew she did herself on occasion. It made her want to reach out and hold her sister's hand, but she was so unsure of the reaction she would get that she held back.

'Why didn't you come to me in the first place?' Simone asked. 'And don't tell me it's because of our small apartment or Jerry's smoking.'

'I…' Brooke broke off. Could she say this and get away with it? Emily's words rang in her ear. *Just do it.* 'Because you've already given up way too much for my sake. I know you never wanted to raise me. How can I ask for anything more after that?'

Simone opened her mouth to protest, but Brooke cut her off.

'You didn't and I get that. You were still a big kid yourself. With grand plans, all of which were cut off the moment Mum and Dad died and you were burdened with a thirteen-year-old. I've done everything in my power to be as independent as I could be since I was old enough to try.'

Simone's face turned paler and paler with every word, until she dropped her chin and stared at her hands. 'I never understood why you married such a buffoon. You were such a smart kid. I thought you must have been in love. But now it's all so clear. You married that cheating bastard…for me?'

Danny's words rang in her ears: *'so many couples nowadays settle for the wrong reasons rather than waiting to find that one right person.'* Brooke shook her hair off her face, but it also gave her a moment to centre herself. This was fast becoming heavy. 'I married him because he was fun, he adored me and he asked.'

'Right. If that's the line you want to spin. Oh, Brooke, you silly sod,' Simone said, but it had none of her usual acidity. 'When Mum and Dad died, it was my decision to take you on, against advice from, well, everyone.'

'Seriously?'

'Hell, yeah. There was talk of sending you to a distant aunt, but there was no way I was going to let that happen.' Simone nodded, sniffed, then shook out her own darker hair. 'But the fact that about the same time I found out I can't have kids of my own didn't help the situation any after that.'

'Oh, Simone,' Brooke said, reaching out and laying a hand over her sister's. When Simone's cool fingers closed around her own she was infinitely glad she hadn't thought about it. She had just followed her instincts and done it. And the sensation of being cocooned in familial love was just beautiful. And infinitely fortifying.

'And there I was, determined to bring up a thirteen-year-old with an attitude problem. It was as if the fates had it in for me big time, by giving me a bratty teenager without all the good stuff before or after it. And then you grew up and got married and were pregnant within five minutes flat. I kind of iced over at that stage. It was the only way I could cope. Why do you think I became a lawyer?'

Simone grinned, sharp incisors making up for the fact that her eyes were brimming with tears. And Brooke lost it. She laughed so hard she had to both clutch a hand to her stomach and wipe away tears.

'Now you know why I'm such a sucker for your kids,' Simone said. 'And I knew Cal never liked me much, but you never let that stop them from being a part of my life. Thank you. Truly.'

Brooke squeezed Simone's hand. 'Does Jerry know?'

'He does. And he loves me anyway. Why else do you think I keep him around?'

'Well,' Brooke said, 'I always thought it had something to do with his tongue piercing, actually.'

'Well, there's always that.' Simone smiled and blinked away any evidence of mistiness. 'Now, what do you need? Money? A job? A place to stay? You know I bought my apartment using the money from the sale of Mum and Dad's house. Half of that is yours, so if you need me to sell I will. Or you can move in, or I can buy you out.'

Brooke thought about it and realised that wasn't what she really needed. She still wanted to take control of her own destiny. And she still believed she could do it.

'What I really need is your support, no matter what happens next.'

Simone blinked, then smiled. 'You've always had it, kiddo. I'll just be sure to remind you as often as I can.'

Later that night, after both the kids were in bed, Danny went searching for Brooke. They had barely had a moment together all day. He hadn't been able to talk to her, to touch her, to keep track of what she might be thinking. Or overthinking as the case likely was. And it had driven him half crazy.

He'd thought himself strong. And true. And able to withstand the mounting pressure of living with her while not being with her. But he'd been kidding himself. Another day like the one he'd just lived through, another day of reliving her kiss and knowing she was merely a room away and he wouldn't cope.

The time had come to put an end to the games, and the sideways glances and the mushrooming possibilities. The time had come to find out what he and Brooke were really about.

He found her standing at the kitchen window, looking out over his dark side yard. She was barefoot, her hair was loose and messy, her clothes hung off her as though they belonged to someone two sizes larger than she was. The fairy lights around the pool beyond played across her skin.

He put his hands into his pockets, took a deep breath and said, 'Hiding in plain sight, I see.'

She turned from the hips. Her hand was at her chest, wrapped tight around something… The locket.

He swallowed. He hadn't even realised she had found his gift, much less opened it and put it on. But she was wearing it now. Close to her heart. Despite the way things had gone the night before, and the way he'd acted that morning, hope surged through him, strong and powerful, until he felt as if he could float on air.

Until she said, 'I'm thinking about moving out.'

And his hope faded like an extinguished match, leaving the swelling hope he had been so determined to ignore just as shrivelled and burnt. He leaned back against the kitchen bench, crossed his arms and used every last ounce of strength to keep his cool. 'And why's that?'

'I got another phone call from the girl from *Sports Scene* today. This story, about us, isn't going away any time soon.'

This story. About them. If that wasn't the most perfect segue, he didn't know what was.

'What if it never goes away,' he said, 'this *story* about us? Would that really be so bad?'

She swallowed. But now her face was shrouded in darkness and he couldn't hope to decipher her reactions to him. 'It's not at all fair on you,' she said.

Meaning she was stubbornly ignoring the fact that the story had basis in truth, hoping it might go away all on its own. It was her *modus operandi*. The reason she had stayed with Cal all those years. But he wasn't Cal. And he wasn't going to let her get away with it.

'Don't bring me into this, Brooke. I can take care of myself. But what about you? Is the thought of the two of us being—'

What? Being together? Lovers? Man and wife? His chest felt so tight, the concepts crashing in on one another until they made a dire whole, but he forced himself to crash through the barrier until he found the words.

'More than friends,' he settled on, then wished he'd delved deeper, given more, but this was all so new to him. 'Is that out of the realm of possibility?'

'Danny, I…I don't know what to say.'

'Then listen,' he said, pushing himself away from the kitchen bench and simply giving in to instinct. If he listened to his head, to his past, to his conscience, he'd never do this. And he had to do this. Now. This was it. His only chance with her. And if he didn't take it, if he didn't throw himself into it with as much vehemence and passion and intent as he had everything else in his life, then he didn't deserve her.

Her sweet chin tilted and her face came into focus as he came ever closer. But she didn't let go of the locket, holding on to it as though it was some kind of talisman.

He took a deep breath through his nose and reached out and took her chin gently in hand. He licked his lips. Slowly. Her gaze trailed downwards, watching the move. Her chest rose and fell. Her eyes darkened. And he knew, no matter how hard she was trying to fight it, she had feelings for him too. It gave him the final push to go completely over the edge.

'Brooke, honey, last night you asked me why I stick by you. I only told you some of the reasons why. But I can't go another day without telling you them all.'

He ran his thumb over her lips, which fell apart and brushed a soft sweet sigh over his skin.

'I stick by you, and I want to stick by you for as long as my arms are strong enough to catch you when you stumble. You were and still are the most gorgeous creature I have ever seen. You make my skin warm, you make my heart leap, and you make me want to slow down and enjoy the spoils of my labour. You are, and always have been, the only one. Brooke, don't you see? You are the last woman I ever want to kiss.'

When she didn't move, didn't turn and didn't flinch, he buried his other hand in her thick blonde hair, pulling her close. And she let him.

He drank in the scent of apples and sunshine. He revelled in the feel of her heavy hair sliding through his fingers. He closed his eyes and let the warmth of her breath against his chest infuse him with such possibility.

Then, no longer able to control himself, he leaned down and replaced his thumb with his mouth, kissing her with all the gentleness he could manage. The soft sweet warmth of her seeping into his very bones and making him feel nothing but her. Her strength and her beauty rolling through him.

Then he tilted her head back and kissed her harder. More thoroughly. This time it was his turn to set the pace. And the pace he required was hot and frantic. He gave everything of himself in that kiss. He didn't hold back. Not a thing.

It was the most terrifying kiss of his life.

Until her hands wound around his neck, her fingers slowly

delving into the hair at the base of his neck, and she kissed him back. All fear fled as he simply lived the pure happiness of finally being able to experience all of her. To hold her, wrap his arms about her and kiss her.

'God, I love you,' Danny murmured against her soft lips, his voice husky, the words spilling from him before he even felt them well up past the lump in his throat.

In return he ended up with a stiffened body in his arms. He took a deep breath and pulled away, only far enough that he could look into her eyes. Brooke was red-faced, as though she hadn't taken a breath since he'd said…what he'd said.

That was the first time he'd ever said those words aloud. And this wasn't exactly the reaction he'd hoped might come about after such a momentous occasion. Singing angels and undulating foundations aside, he'd expected it to be kind of a nice thing to finally get to experience.

But instead he was facing a woman so wound up he thought she might spontaneously combust. He felt so much pent-up…everything, he might just join her.

Instead he let her go and paced, pulling his hands through his hair, trying to negate the pain in his gut. When he stopped pacing they faced each other across the kitchen like a pair of gunslingers. Danny wondered who would flinch first.

He wasn't all that surprised when it turned out to be him. The stubborn little miss could have stood there for a week if he hadn't made the first move.

'Brooke, stop acting like I just kicked your cat and talk to me.'

When she looked ready to fight him even on that he turned and walked away. He'd given as much as he could give. He'd given her time, space, support, and he'd given her his heart. If she wasn't even going to give an inch…

'You don't love me, Danny.'

That snapped him out of whatever last bubble of hope he'd enclosed himself in. Just like that, he felt it dissolve, fade away, leaving him raw and open and pulsing from head to toe. He turned back to face her. 'How can you possibly claim to know what's going on in my heart?'

'I haven't… I can't be what you want me to be, Danny. I just can't. I can't be tied to you like some kind of pathetic Rapunzel, clinging to you from my tower through the need for survival.'

'No,' he said, 'don't you even think about laying that on me. Unlike others in your life before me, I have no plans to hold you back, Brooke. Ever. I want you to do exactly what you need to do to be happy. But I'm also no longer afraid to tell you that being with you is the one thing I need to make me happy.'

'Well, bully for you,' she scoffed, looking away for the first time.

'I'm being nothing but honest with you Brooke.'

Her eyes roved back, connecting with his. It gave him such a head rush he had to scrunch his toes in his shoes to keep blood moving through the rest of him.

'Well then,' she said, 'I'm obviously much better at coping with pretty lies.'

Her chest heaved, her eyes flashed, and he knew that there was nothing he could say or do to change her mind. To make her see. He could stand there and tell her he loved her until he was blue in the face and she wouldn't yield. She wouldn't believe.

At that he told himself enough was enough. He'd tried. He'd loved her and it hadn't been enough. He could simply give no more.

'I understand why you can't trust me,' he said, his voice weary. 'I really do.'

'But I—'

'Brooke. Don't. If you trusted me, we wouldn't be having this conversation.'

Was he really about to do this? To say this? The ridiculous thing was—while she stood there, spitting mad at him— having shared his feelings hadn't lessened their impact one bit. It hadn't taken the edge off them either. He fell in love with her more each and every moment in her company and he knew he would continue to do so every moment she was in his line of sight, every moment she was in his thoughts. And it just hurt too damn much.

'Brooke, I think you are on the money. I think the time has come for you to find your own place.'

Her mouth dropped open; she blinked up at him. As though she had been expecting him to put a stop to her again. But if that was what she wanted, she was going to have to tell him. She was going to have to say the words.

'Are you *asking* me to leave?' she said, her face pale, her cheeks blotchy and pink. It took all of Danny's strength not to take everything back and just promise to wait for her as long as she needed him to. He'd waited eight years already…

But those had been eight years thinking she'd never be his. Of loving her from afar. Now there was nothing standing in his way bar her inability to fully trust him.

The damage had been done over years and years of other people letting her down. But his love wasn't enough to heal her. And a guy could only be so honourable before he became a fool.

'I can't do this any more, Brooke,' he said, telling it like it was and hating every second of it. But it had to be done. 'I can no longer bear to see you in my kitchen of a morning in your crumpled clothes and messy hair and smudged eyeliner. I can't think of you sleeping three rooms away while my body aches for you. I can't wonder and wait in hope that you might one day come around to loving me back. Slowly but surely it's going to quite simply kill me.'

He allowed himself one last taste of her. He reached out and tucked a moist strand of hair behind her ear, then wiped his thumb gently beneath each eye, her warm tears shining along its length. He leant in and placed a kiss atop her head and closed his eyes and drank in her soft feminine scent and imagined how good they could have been together.

Then, as he pulled away, he felt a steel trap close around his heart. A fortified trap with an unbreakable combination lock and no key. But it didn't matter. He would need no key. No other woman would ever be able to touch his heart the way she had.

'Right,' she said. 'I see.' She nodded. Her chin jutting forward, her hot green eyes raw with pain. And then tears began to stream down her cheeks. She wiped them away with fast furious swipes of her hands.

'I'll give you time off tomorrow to start looking for a new place,' he said, and even he heard the ice in his voice.

'Fine,' she said. 'Tomorrow. I'll start looking for a new place. Maybe in Emerald near Beau's school. That would be good. Still far enough away to give us some anonymity.'

And still near me, he thought, but he knew he was being fanciful. If she really wanted to be that near to him she would dig in her heels and stay. And allow herself to love him back.

'That's sounds ideal,' he said, his voice somehow calm and clear while she seemed to fall apart right in front of him. 'I'll even help you look if you need me to. I'll help you set yourself up. I'll help you in any way you need. Always. You know that, right?'

'But I can't stay,' she said, nodding, almost trying to convince herself as much as she was him.

'No, Brooke. You can't stay. But you don't really need to either. Beau has a new school, you have a new job, and enough money coming in to get your own place. You're ready.'

Ready for the bright future she deserved. But it had taken him to admit to himself and to her that he loved her, and for her to deny him to his face, to realise that he didn't have a place in it.

And he never had.

CHAPTER ELEVEN

THE NEXT MORNING Brooke found herself walking through a small three-bedroom cottage in Emerald with Danny and Lily.

It was the third rental place they had seen that morning; it was well within her means as she was getting a good salary working for Danny, it had a lovely big yard, stupendous views and good heating.

But somehow she couldn't feel excited. All she felt was empty. She realised that she hadn't felt that way since the day she had fainted on Danny's office floor. Somehow the past weeks had filled the well. She'd been recharged. Refreshed. At Danny's. With Danny. Because of Danny.

But now, after crying herself quietly to sleep some time around dawn, she once more felt numb. Worse than numb. She felt…wrong. All wrong.

'Can I go play with the toys in the girl's room?' Lily called out.

Brooke reached into her handbag for Lily's favourite book. 'Here, sweetheart. Take *Olivia* and go sit on the girl's bed and be very careful.'

Lily made no promises as she ran off to the room filled with toys.

Brooke remained in the kitchen, looking through the

window at Danny, who was outside with the estate agent, probably talking over important things like plumbing and contracts. As though he was the man in her life.

She crossed her arms and breathed out a soft regretful sigh. Danny. Who the night before had held her in his arms and told her he loved her.

In that moment, as those three little words had pierced her hazy subconscious, her body had begged her to give in and just let him. Her instincts had led her to sway to him, to continue the kiss that had bruised her mouth and warmed her heart, until her conditioning had her rejecting the very thought. History told her that she had done nothing to deserve to be loved so fiercely.

And so, in a panic, she had thrown it back in his face.

She'd hurt him. There was no doubt that was what her hesitation and her denial had done to him. She'd seen it in his eyes. She had never before seen him so vulnerable. She had never before seen *any* man so vulnerable. And seeing her big, strong, strapping Danny Finch that way just made her heart ache.

It ached still. Now. All these hours later. She wished she could put a stop to it. Or even a name to it. Or take a pill and make the ache go away, the slow seeping ache that made her bones feel cold. This sensation that her Danny was out there in the world loving her, and she was digging in her toes and letting it slip by.

Her Danny. The man in her life. The thought caught hold and dug deep. So deep. Deeper than she'd ever felt anything in her whole life.

He crouched down, his ubiquitous black suit stretching across the best butt she had ever laid eyes on. Emily was not wrong there. The estate agent with his paunch and bald patch and ill-fitting mushroom-coloured suit did his best to crouch down as well. He nodded as Danny patted at a patch of grass. She couldn't even hope to wonder what he was so worried about out there. But the fact was he was still worried about her.

He stood, brushing off his hands. And then, as though he could feel her watching him, he turned and pinned her with a warm stare.

Her heart thundered in an instant, knocking against her ribs so hard it bruised. But it was a good kind of hurt. Like intense pleasure and intense happiness all rolled into one. So intense all other hurt was simply washed away on its strong tide.

And then he smiled. Barely. A slight lifting of the right corner of his beautiful mouth. The faint crinkling of the skin around his eyes. She could almost hear him telling her everything was going to be okay. And she almost believed him.

But once again it became too much, she was too unaccustomed to deciphering these feelings bombarding her. She spun on her heel and headed off to find Lily. She was, unbelievably, sitting on the little girl's bed reading her *Olivia* book.

'So what do you think, Lily?' she asked, reaching out and running a hand over her daughter's curls.

'Of what?'

Brooke plucked a fallen pink feather from the bed and put it in her handbag, where it joined a dozen others. 'Of the house. Do you think we could make our new home here? This could be your bedroom.'

Lily stopped kicking the side of the bed and looked at her. 'But I have a bedroom at Danny's.'

'Don't you think it would be nice to have a place of our own? Just you, me and Beau?'

'And Buckley?'

'Well, no, Buckley would stay with Danny, but we could visit any time we pleased.' She wondered as she said the words how true they were. Could she really visit Danny? Knowing how drawn to him she was, how much his kisses affected her, how much she cared. And knowing how much she'd hurt him.

Lily opened her mouth, then shut it again. And her bottom lip began to tremble. Her tiny shoulders slumped and her face dropped. Brooke didn't quite know what to say.

And then Danny poked his head around the door. 'Hi,' he said, his voice husky in the mid-morning quiet.

'Hi,' she said, the word tearing from her through a throat so tight she realised she suddenly felt like crying. Like pouting and slumping her shoulders. Just like Lily.

'John's gone out to his car,' Danny said. 'He's giving us a few minutes to have a look around on our own.' He turned to Lily. 'Now, this room would be just perfect for you.'

But Lily was not convinced. She was off the bed in a flash and then she threw herself into Danny's arms and sobbed. Just sobbed.

Brooke watched in mute amazement. Though she knew exactly what Lily was feeling. It was as though her daughter was living out her own compelling desire to cling to Danny and never let go.

Lily's feather boa slid off her shoulders and fluttered to the floor. Brooke stood and picked it up, moving to Danny, unable to avoid his eyes which were boring into hers. The hurt and surprise and the care warring behind his dark irises reached out to her, lassoing her, drawing her to him as surely as if he'd told her he loved her again.

'Here, sweetheart,' Brooke said, placing the boa around Lily's shoulders like a security blanket. But Lily just squealed and shrugged it off. For the first time since her dad had died, she shrugged it off.

Overwhelmed by the escalating collection of emotions weighing upon her, Brooke said, 'We'd...I'm sorry, but I'd better take her home.'

Home. To Danny's.

He nodded, but didn't give her over. He kept patting Lily's curls and let her cling to him, tears flowing over his beautiful suit jacket, but he didn't give a damn.

He did hold out a hand. And Brooke took it. And they left the darling cottage, the kind of place she would have thought perfect had she gone looking only a few short weeks earlier.

They walked to his car, snuggled tight like a family who, though they loved one another dearly, still knew they were on the verge of breaking apart.

'Stay,' Danny said on a whisper, even though Lily was fast asleep upstairs at his house. 'Lucille can handle things today.'

Stay. He'd only meant for her to stay at his house and take the rest of the day off. But for a brief moment Brooke had thought he'd meant stay...forever, and she'd felt a shot of pure bliss travel through her. Bliss, confidence, happiness. And love.

Everything finally made sense to her. She loved him. She really, truly was in love with Danny Finch. He filled her soul. He made her laugh. He made her feel safe and he made her feel sexy. If she made him feel even half of what she felt for him, then she had no doubt that he truly was in love with her. Her Danny. The man in her life. And the thought of pushing all of that out of her life so that she could take on some mission to be her own person suddenly didn't make any sense to her.

She wasn't her own person. Not in the sense she was thinking she ought to be. She was Simone's sister. She was Beau and Lily's mother. She was Cal's widow. And she would be for evermore.

But she was also a woman who was loved. By Danny. She could be his some girl… This could be their some day… And there was simply no other way to go but forward. In order to do that, she had to risk the most important friendship in her life for the chance of the love of a lifetime.

As though he sensed her struggle and simply couldn't be there to see himself lose again, Danny gave her one last look—dark, hot, confused…and torn—and then he turned and walked out the front door.

Brooke's feet dug into the hardwood floor, but her heart had had enough of being second best. She ran out the front door after him. 'Danny, wait.'

He turned at his car. 'What's up?'

Brooke took a deep breath. She had so much to say she had no idea where to begin. 'Lily doesn't want to leave,' she said, taking baby steps.

He blinked. And simply gave her the space to say what she needed to say.

'And, though I haven't broached it with him, I know Beau feels the same way. They…we've come to love living here. With you.'

He shifted his stance slightly, lounging against the car. But this time she knew he wasn't as cool as he seemed. It was a self-defence mechanism. He was preparing himself to deal with whatever new difficulty she was intending to put in his way.

'You don't want the cottage, then, I take it?'

She shook her head. 'I don't want the cottage.'

'Because you don't want any cottage?'

She nodded. 'No cottage will do.'

'Brooke, what are you trying to tell me?' he asked.

He was so good with words. Always had been. He dealt in words day in and day out. She wasn't nearly so proficient.

So, instead of finding words, she took two more steps—
short steps, but momentous steps—until she was looking up
into his eyes. And then she slowly eased up on tiptoe, her
whole body shaking under the weight of what she was about
to do. She placed her hands on his shoulders and then she
kissed him.

A soft, sweet kiss that started at her heart and spread
outward, sending rays of love through her limbs, wrapping her
in hope and certainty that this man was worth every single
speck of love she had inside her.

When she pulled away, his eyes were closed. They slowly
flickered open, the dark depths of his golden eyes gleaming
with molten heat.

'So that's what you were trying to say,' he said with an in-
dulgent smile.

'There's more,' she said, dropping her hands and twining
them together in front of her.

'I can't wait.' He reached out and tucked a strand of hair
behind her ear, letting his fingers trail down her neck before
pulling away. That simple touch gave her more encouragement to go forward than he could have known.

'Danny,' she said, her voice ragged and soft in the wide
open space of his front drive, the sound carrying no further
than his ears. But she didn't need it to. This was her private
story to tell. And he was the only audience she needed in
order to tell it.

'Yes, Brooke.'

'I think I love you too.'

A shaft of hot breath shot from Danny's lungs, flicking her
hair off her face. She breathed in deep, revelling in his scent,
his warmth and the certainty that he had caught up. He had
caught up and he believed her.

'You think…?' he repeated, his mouth kicking up into a warm half smile.

'I know,' she shot back before she could second-guess, overthink or let any old issues of mistrust surface and spoil everything. Never again would they hold sway. Not if it meant losing what she had. Here. Now. With this man.

'I've loved you for years,' she told him. Her voice shook, but she didn't let that stop her. 'You have always been important to me. You've kept me sane and centred and made me feel like I had a friend when things were going wrong in my life. Someone I could count on to stand up for me no matter what. But I've come to love the way you are with my kids, and the way you would tear Simone to pieces if I ever said the word. I even love your egotistical determination that you are always right.'

His smile broadened and oh, what a smile it was. He reached out and hooked a finger into the belt line of her jeans and slowly tugged her closer. She let her hands land upon his broad chest, her fingers curling into the fabric of his black shirt.

'You do?' he asked, his voice rumbling through her.

'Nah,' she said, 'I hate that you always think you're right. It drives me up the wall.'

His smile became a grin, such a beautiful, sexy, mesmerising grin, she found she could barely breathe.

He gave her one last tug until she was flush up against him. 'If you're saying what I think you're saying, you're simply going to have to get used to that.'

Her hands wrapped around his neck, running along the soft, perfectly straight line of hair at his collar, her confidence growing with each and every touch. Each and every moment she looked into his eyes and saw for herself the love he had professed for her.

'I am saying what you think I'm saying,' she said. 'I'm in

love with you, Danny. And, try as you might to kick me out, I'm not leaving. I'm never leaving.'

'Just try it,' he said.

His words infused her with strength and power and confidence and self-belief until she was sure she was floating a good three inches off the ground.

'I'm sorry about yesterday, I really am, I—'

He held a finger to her lips. 'Yesterday is long gone. What's past is past, remember.'

'That's right.' She smiled up at him, his finger trailing across her lips. 'Good motto, that one. Maybe I'll take that one instead.'

'Mmm,' Danny said. 'Now, stop yabbering and tell me again why you love me. Does it have anything to do with my brains, my success or my... what was the other part?'

Brooke grinned and leaned into him. 'Your unsurpassed good looks? Sure, why not?'

Danny's golden gaze took a few moments to trail over her face, as though he was memorising her exact expression.

'I quite like your hands too, actually,' she said, and his mouth kicked into a sexy half smile. 'And that dimple drives me crazy. And right now I'm struggling not to stop talking and just kiss you forever.'

Danny's smile softened, became gentle. And she realised he was trembling. How she was able to make a man like this tremble in her arms, she had no idea. But she was not going to question it ever again. She was simply going to live it. And love it right on back.

'So stop yabbering and just do it,' he said.

Brooke didn't need to be asked twice. She leant in and kissed him. And he kissed her. Pulling her tight, wrapping her in his strong embrace and thanking her and worshipping her and loving her all at the same time. It was beautiful and sensual and intensely private. Just like the man in her arms. The man in her life. The man in her heart.

When the kiss ended as naturally as it had begun, she leant back ever so slightly, just enough to make sure his attention was fully on her. 'But I have no intention of letting you think you're right all the time.'

'How about this one last time, then?' he said, his eyes smouldering so hot she could barely hear his words over the blood rushing in her head.

'Stay,' he said, and this time she knew exactly what he meant. 'Stay. Live with me. Let me love you as much as I have always wanted to love you. And marry me.'

'Yes,' she said, without a second's hesitation. 'I'll marry you, Danny Finch.'

He pulled her into his arms before the last word had left her mouth. He lifted her off the ground for real, enveloping her in his strength until she didn't know where she began and he ended. Maybe that was because there was no such fine line.

They were some pair. Stubborn, damaged, healed and so very much in love. And neither of them made it back to the office that day.

The next six weeks flew by in a whirl. Danny had landed himself a first round draft pick, sold a baseball player in a ten-million-dollar deal, and the four of them had watched his footy team win a grand final.

But now life had settled down. Her life.

Brooke lay back on a Lilo in the pool, letting the sun warm her face. She opened the Sunday morning newspaper to find a picture of her and Danny on their wedding day.

They hadn't sold their story to the highest bidder. They

hadn't even tried to hide the fact they were getting married. They had simply got on with their lives and done it, with a minimum of fuss, a maximum of love and fun and laughter and tears. And afterwards they'd released one picture to the world.

In the picture she was looking down, her hair was loose and probably too messy for a bride, but she hadn't minded one bit. She'd been on cloud nine all day and the hairdresser could have put her hair in pigtails and she wouldn't have cared. A beautiful champagne lace bodice clung tight to her curves. Her simple pavé set wedding ring glittered beautifully, even in the black-and-white picture. And Danny smiled down at her, his love radiating out of the picture so that she could feel it even now.

In the newspaper the printed picture was surrounded by emailed and written messages from dozens of people neither she nor Danny had ever met. People wishing them well. Wishing her well. People who she now hoped would have a sense of closure on the tale of Brooke Findlay, while Brooke Finch began a new life.

Beau jumped into the pool, screaming out, 'Dive-bomb!' a second before he hit the water, covering Brooke in so much water the newspaper all but turned to pulp in her hands. She threw it on to the hot tiles beside the pool.

Danny swum up beside her, treading water, his strong, tanned forearms resting along her thigh, his little finger stroking her gently, sending shivers of pleasure along her length. 'Hey, gorgeous,' he said.

She spluttered and spat wet hair out of her mouth. 'You're nuts. I look like a drowned rat.'

'Fishing for compliments again, are we? I thought that marrying you and pledging my undying love would be enough, but no. You need reassurance each and every day for the rest of time? Then I'm afraid that's what you're going to get. But first…'

He kicked off the bottom of the pool, then tugged at the side of the Lilo and she had just enough time to take a shallow breath before she was dunked. She came up for air, pulling her saturated hair off her face and opening her eyes to the spring sunshine to find Danny leaning against the side of the pool, innocent as you please.

'I owe you,' she said, slowly swimming his way. 'You're not going to see it coming, but one day, and soon, I'm going to repay you for that.'

Danny stuck out a foot, wrapped his leg around her and dragged her to him. Her hands grabbed on to his slick shoulders, her breath shot from her lungs at the look in his eyes.

'I await the day with bated breath,' he said, before pulling her in for a slow tender kiss.

'Danny! Mum!' Lily called out from the other side of the pool, where Beau was watching her swim with floats. 'Look at me. I'm doing breath-stroke.'

Danny laughed and, letting his hand slowly trail around Brooke's waist, he swam to join her kids. Her happy kids who loved Danny almost as much as she did.

Brooke sniffed and, before she knew it, hot tears were pouring out of her wide open eyes, mixing with the salt of the pool water.

Over the past weeks she'd come to realise that she was a crying type of girl after all. For tears were not only for toddlers with scraped knees, guys who'd had too much to drink and guests on Oprah. They were also for women who loved their families so much they didn't give a hoot if the whole darned world knew it.

REQUEST YOUR FREE BOOKS!
2 FREE NOVELS PLUS 2
FREE GIFTS!

HARLEQUIN ROMANCE®

From the Heart, For the Heart

YES! Please send me 2 FREE Harlequin Romance® novels and my 2 FREE gifts. After receiving them, if I don't wish to receive any more books, I can return the shipping statement marked "cancel." If I don't cancel, I will receive 4 brand-new novels every month and be billed just $3.57 per book in the U.S., or $4.05 per book in Canada, plus 25¢ shipping and handling per book and applicable taxes, if any*. That's a savings of over 15% off the cover price! I understand that accepting the 2 free books and gifts places me under no obligation to buy anything. I can always return a shipment and cancel at any time. Even if I never buy another book from Harlequin, the two free books and gifts are mine to keep forever.

114 HDN EEV7 314 HDN EEWK

Name	(PLEASE PRINT)

Address	Apt.

City	State/Prov.	Zip/Postal Code

Signature (if under 18, a parent or guardian must sign)

Mail to the **Harlequin Reader Service®:**
IN U.S.A.: P.O. Box 1867, Buffalo, NY 14240-1867
IN CANADA: P.O. Box 609, Fort Erie, Ontario L2A 5X3

Not valid to current Harlequin Romance subscribers.

Want to try two free books from another line?
Call 1-800-873-8635 or visit www.morefreebooks.com.

* Terms and prices subject to change without notice. NY residents add applicable sales tax. Canadian residents will be charged applicable provincial taxes and GST. This offer is limited to one order per household. All orders subject to approval. Credit or debit balances in a customer's account(s) may be offset by any other outstanding balance owed by or to the customer. Please allow 4 to 6 weeks for delivery.

Your Privacy: Harlequin is committed to protecting your privacy. Our Privacy Policy is available online at www.eHarlequin.com or upon request from the Reader Service. From time to time we make our lists of customers available to reputable firms who may have a product or service of interest to you. If you would prefer we not share your name and address, please check here. ☐

HR07

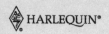

Charlie fell in love with Rose Kaufman
before he even met her, through stories her
husband, Joe, used to tell. When Joe is killed
in the trenches, Charlie helps Rose through
her grief and they make a new life together.
But for Charlie, a question remains—can
love be as true the second time around?
Only one woman can answer that....

Look for

The Soldier and
the Rose

by

Linda Barrett

Available November wherever you buy books.

I ♥ HARLEQUIN® *Presents*

BROUGHT TO YOU BY FANS OF
HARLEQUIN PRESENTS.

We are its editors and authors
and biggest fans—and we'd
love to hear from YOU!

Subscribe today to our online blog at
www.iheartpresents.com